"I think I'd better go home now,"

Sabrina murmured, but found herself leaning toward Michael, instead of pulling away.

His voice was barely a whisper. "Yes, I think it's best that you leave."

Without conscious thought she stepped toward him and heard his sharp indrawn breath. One hand slid around to cup the back of her head and bring her gently but inexorably closer.

The moment she felt his mouth on hers, her body seemed to melt and go up in flames at the same time. Like a moment she'd been waiting for forever. And yet she seemed to know his kiss already, know the shape of his lips with the intimacy of a lover. As their tongues entwined she shuddered with an intensity of feelings that went beyond pleasure, to become almost excruciating. She clung tighter as a little moan escaped her throat.

Michael broke away abruptly.

What were they doing? Shocked at her own instinctive, shameless response, Sabrina moved quickly backward.

Michael's voice was firm, bearing only a slight, betraying trace of raggedness. "It would be useless to deny that I'm attracted to you, but it won't go any further, I can promise you that."

His face became cold. "I can't afford a sexual harassment suit."

Debra Carroll is really two people: Carol Bruce-Thomas and Debra McCarthy-Anderson. Friends forever, five years ago the pair decided they wanted to do something new and interesting with their lives. Rather like Mickey Rooney to Judy Garland, one said to the other, "I know, let's write a romance!" They set a five-year goal to sell to Harlequin. Along the way, they published two romance novels under the name of Rachel Vincer with Meteor Books. And then, with only days to spare in the five-year deadline and just before Christmas, Harlequin phoned and offered them a contract. *Man under the Mistletoe* is their second book for Temptation. Look for their next novel, *To Catch a Thief,* on sale in March 1996.

Deb and Carol would like to wish you all the best of the holiday season.

Books by Debra Carroll

HARLEQUIN TEMPTATION

526—OBSESSION

MAN UNDER THE MISTLETOE

Debra Carroll

Harlequin Books

TORONTO • NEW YORK • LONDON
AMSTERDAM • PARIS • SYDNEY • HAMBURG
STOCKHOLM • ATHENS • TOKYO • MILAN
MADRID • WARSAW • BUDAPEST • AUCKLAND

To Bruce and Mark
for their patience, support, understanding
and occasionally love

ISBN 0-373-25668-X

MAN UNDER THE MISTLETOE

This edition published by arrangement with Harlequin Books S.A.

Printed in U.S.A.

1

"WELL, HELLO, *breakfast!*" Sabrina whispered through a mouth filled with straight pins as she leaned toward the inside of Worth's main display window.

Her gaze followed a tall man striding past on the sidewalk and tracked him like radar. Sharp prickles of pain shot through her lower lip when she pressed her face against the plate glass to keep him in sight.

"Ouch!"

She snatched the pins out of her mouth with the hand that had been holding her large dressmaker shears. The scissors landed with a heavy thunk, points-down in the wooden floor, a millimeter from the toe of her black loafers.

Undeterred, Sabrina pressed her face to the window again, but he had disappeared.

"*Damn.* I hadn't finished looking yet."

With a sigh, she bent down to pry the scissors from the parquet, then stood back to survey her work.

Against the backdrop of a tropical moon shimmering over a deep blue ocean, a tall palm tree bent in a graceful arch over two reclining figures. The female mannequin had her head thrown back, while the lips of her male counterpart hovered mere inches from the exposed curve of her throat.

Both were clad in the skimpiest of beachwear, a new line from Gaultier. Pretty hot stuff for Worth's. Would she get away with it? Her immediate boss, Jonathan Kent, had approved the sketch, which meant that somehow or other he'd managed to sell the idea to the stuffed shirts upstairs. But that didn't mean they wouldn't squawk when they saw the finished window display.

All that remained was to add the sand that was in the stockroom. Slipping behind the backdrop, she opened the small door to the main sales floor and stepped out of the display window just in time to see *him* walk through the massive revolving doors of Worth's.

Be still my beating heart.

He paused just inside the carved stone archway framing the main Yonge Street entrance and slowly scanned the vast, quiet store.

Frozen to the spot, Sabrina could only stare at Mr. Tall, Dark and Drop-Dead Stunning.

Even among the well-heeled clientele of Worth's, this guy stood out. That fabulous navy suit was two thousand dollars' worth of Italian tailoring, if she was any judge. Even from a distance she could tell the quality of the fabric and the impeccable cut.

But it was what filled out the suit that made it look so fabulous. Over six feet of your average lean, broad-shouldered... hunkahunka burnin' love...

She grinned. Okay, so she was acting like the village idiot, but so what? A woman didn't get a break like this every day.

Her fingers itched to grab a sketch pad. But did she have the talent to get across that aura of command and purpose he radiated, even from this distance? Could pen and ink hope to do justice to the hard, well-exercised body evident beneath the tailored suit?

He looked somewhere in his mid-thirties. And he wasn't just a pretty face, either. Her eyes traced his lean, hard features, the square determined jaw. The face of a man who could handle any situation life might throw his way. And he looked as if life had given him plenty of practice.

The way his black hair waved back, thick and luxuriant, from his high forehead, already seemed familiar. She imagined the firm pencil strokes that would capture those well-shaped dark brows, contracting slightly now as his gaze swept over the nearly empty store. But it wasn't the usual "where the heck am I?" look. No, he was too intense for that.

Suddenly he strode off down the red carpet of the central aisle, with the smooth, athletic movements of a man in top physical condition.

With a sigh, she turned and locked the door behind her. Enough drooling. It was time to get back to work.

Cutting through the perfume sales area toward the stockroom, she came out onto the main aisle just as Mr. Gorgeous walked by. Another little thrill of pleasure went through her. What luck—they seemed to be heading in the same direction.

From thirty feet behind, she followed him past the oak-paneled counters and softly lit displays as he walked slowly down the aisle, his head turning to scan first one side, then the other.

"Excuse me. Could you please tell us where to find mothballs, dear?"

With her gaze fixed on the tall man up ahead, Sabrina didn't see the two elderly ladies until she almost walked into them. She stopped abruptly to find two pairs of hopeful eyes peering up at her through matching bifocals. It was a rude awakening.

"Mothballs... That'll be in housewares," she said automatically. "Fifth floor. When you get off the escalator, turn to your right."

She could only manage an abstracted nod as the women thanked her and toddled away, her attention still focused on the handsome stranger.

He had pulled up short by an unattended sales desk piled with home spa products. What could be commanding such keen interest? Could he be in the market for a herbal body wrap?

Her gaze ran slowly over his broad shoulders and down his back, over narrow hips and all the way down the length of his legs. Heaven knows, he didn't need one, but she'd be glad to give him a body wrap. With her whole body.

Her mouth curved in a small, wicked grin and she began walking down the aisle again. Indulging in a little sexual fantasy was a delightful way to break up the day, but it was time to get that sand. She had too much else to get done before five.

As luck would have it, he was moving again, too, just a few feet ahead of her. Suddenly he stopped at one of the jewelry counters, leaned over and rattled the locked doors behind the display.

She stopped in her tracks. What on earth was he up to? Should she go up and ask him if he needed some help? The store was hardly overrun with salesclerks. Wednesday afternoons were notoriously slow; in fact, most weekdays were slow, but this was ridiculous. *All* the staff couldn't possibly be on their break at the same time.

Over in the camera department a couple of clerks stood chatting, but except for the far corner, where Ladies' Wear was having a sale, most of the counters stood deserted.

He began moving again, and without even thinking she slowly followed. Something about his manner was beginning to seem peculiar. He prowled on through the jewelry department, past the racks of tasteful costume pearls, with an alert and watchful air.

Suddenly he stopped dead beside a display case where the real thing glittered against deep blue velvet.

A grim smile tightened one corner of his mouth and she followed his contemptuous gaze. Lying between a box of credit card slips and the cash register she could see the unmistakable sparkle of diamonds.

Quickly he stepped behind the counter, picked up the diamonds and slipped them into his pocket.

"Oh my God, he's a thief!" The words fell out of Sabrina's mouth in a shocked gasp as the man continued brazenly on his way.

Panic set her heart pounding as her head whipped around, searching in vain for one of the security staff, then turned back to find only the empty aisle.

Oh, no . . . No! She *had* to find him. The stuff in that counter was worth more than her job if she let him get away with it.

In desperation, she hurried toward the only busy spot on the main sales floor. How far could he have gone and how hard could he be to find? After all, the man's looks had caused her to practically amputate her toe at the first sight of him. And in Women's Hosiery he'd be pretty hard to miss.

A crowd of short society matrons clustered around the bins of panty hose. The two-for-one sale had them elbowing each other out of the way.

This was hopeless. He'd tower over all these women. If he were here she'd have spotted him in a minute.

As she pushed through the crowd, craning her neck to scan the surroundings for his dark head, she jumped up to get a better view and landed hard on her anklebone. Wincing at the pain, she limped away from the crowd. Well, she was no Baryshnikov, that was for sure.

She was no Nancy Drew, either. She'd lost him. And now she'd have to report the theft and that the culprit had got away. Her head would be on the chopping block for this one and, when all was said and done, it really wasn't her problem. She was in Display, not Security. But at the same time, it was her responsibility as an employee to stop him from getting away.

All at once she felt a surge of anger and disappointment. He had such an aura of power and control about him, he had no right turning out to be a slimy, low-down thief.

Turning abruptly, she cannoned head-on into a solid male chest. Something pushed painfully into the tip of her nose, and she drew back to see a tiny diamond pinning the bold floral silk tie she'd been following for the past fifteen minutes.

Shocked by the impact, she drew a deep breath. The warm woodsy scent of his cologne flooded her senses. Then she stepped back and looked up into a pair of the bluest eyes she had ever seen. Deep azure, as clear as a summer sky. *Oh, my.*

Her heart did a frantic somersault and she reeled backward, but he reached out to steady her, his hands gripping her upper arms.

"I'm sorry. Are you all right?"

She didn't know what was more disturbing: the sound of his low voice, the feel of his strong fingers gripping her flesh or those impossibly blue eyes boring into hers. She strained away from him and he quickly let her go.

"I'm fine," she blurted out, stepping abruptly backward. But she was shaken up, no doubt about it. How could her libido betray her like this?

"Are you sure . . ." His glance fell to the store ID badge that swung from a silver chain around her slender neck. ". . . Miss Cates? You look like you're about to pass out."

His gaze swept their surroundings, then before she knew what was happening, his fingers had curled decisively around her upper arm again, and he was leading her toward a nearby display dais. The firm pressure of his grip indicated she should sink down onto the convenient ledge.

"Here. Why don't you sit down for a minute?"

Sit down? She'd be lucky if she didn't pass out. When his warm, hard fingers closed around her arm, the tingling electricity had spread right down to her toes.

"No! I'll be all right." She pulled away from him as if she were fighting for her very life. *Calm down!*

"Are you sure?" He fixed her with a doubtful, impatient look.

"I'm just a little winded." If not completely truthful, it was a convenient excuse for her rapid, heavy breathing.

"I'm not surprised. You came at me as if the devil himself were after you. You really shouldn't be running around the store, Miss Cates. It looks so unprofessional and could be very dangerous."

Her jaw dropped in disbelief, shock dispelling some of the sexual awareness. "I beg your pardon?"

Of all the nerve! To stand there with stolen jewelry in his pocket and have the unmitigated gall to lecture *her* on her professionalism!

"That's better. You have a little more color in your face now." His firm mouth curved in the smallest of perfunctory smiles.

Color? She'd give him color! He might be a foot taller and outweigh her by eighty pounds or so, but she wasn't about to let him get away with this.

"Excuse me, I have to get back to work," she said tersely. She turned on her heel and walked away, although she wasn't planning on going far.

After a cautious backward glance to make sure he was heading in the opposite direction, she ducked into the next aisle, then crept along after him, keeping herself concealed.

Thank God she'd found him. And this time she'd better hang on to him. Her heart pounding, she tried to beat back the waves of disappointment. Not only was he a crook, but an arrogant one, too.

The chase had taken on a vivid air of unreality. But the reality was that if he left the store with the goods, she'd have to go out there after him. She'd have to ask this six foot of dangerous-looking male, who appeared the epitome of affluence, to "step back inside again please, sir." As if he would just meekly comply.

Her gaze raced frantically around the store again in despair. *Still* no security personnel in sight.

The thief had come to a stop, his attention on something she couldn't see. Leaning over the counter beside her, she snatched up the phone by the cash register and punched the number of the security office. Twirling the cord around her finger, she listened to the nonstop ringing with growing impatience.

And then all at once her man was on the move again. She kept her eyes riveted on him, not even daring to blink for fear of losing him. Suddenly he passed behind the escalators and disappeared from view.

Slamming down the phone, she raced after him, seething with frustration. This was ridiculous. Where were Chuck and the rest of his security staff?

She stopped in her tracks, catching sight of him again over in Women's Coats. He seemed to be watching a salesclerk handle a transaction. The quality of his absorption was baffling. A fur coat lay on the counter, but even he couldn't expect to get away with that. After a moment he moved on.

Never taking her eyes off the broad-shouldered figure making his way down the aisle, she darted over to the clerk.

"Call Security," she said rapidly. "Get them down here right away."

"What?"

She turned impatiently to see the woman and her customer staring at her as if she'd gone mad. "Just call them. Now."

Without waiting to see if the clerk would do as she was told, Sabrina hurried after him as he turned a corner and disappeared from view again. Breaking into a near run, she rounded the turn, slowing down when she saw him just ahead, picking up a coat that had fallen to the floor and putting it back on the hanger.

Cool fingers curled around her elbow, halting her abruptly.

"There you are, Sabrina. I've been looking everywhere for you."

She let out her breath in frustration, turning reluctantly to the lanky blond boy smiling down at her. Even if he was Worth's heir apparent, he was the last person she wanted to see right now.

"Colin, I can't stop and chat. I'll talk to you later."

A petulant frown crossed his narrow face. "Oh, come on. You've been saying that for two days."

When she tried to pull away, his grip tightened.

"Let go of my arm."

At her stern look the frown changed to a coaxing smile. "Come on, Sabrina."

"Colin, stop it. You can ask until you're blue in the face, and the answer will still be the same."

At seventeen, long after the rest of his classmates at St. Andrew's School for Boys, Nature had finally caught up with Colin Worth. Since last year, he had shot up half a foot and finally discovered the opposite sex. Unfortunately for her, she was the chosen target.

"Tell me, young man, are you going to stand there all day?" An elderly woman with blue rinsed hair stood behind him as he blocked the aisle. She hoisted her furled umbrella and prodded Colin smartly in the back.

He flashed the woman a winning smile, then shot Sabrina a cheeky wink as he pulled her out of the way.

"C'mon. I bet you'll have a good time if you just stop being so silly about this age thing."

His blue eyes smiled down at her with disconcerting confidence. Why couldn't she get it through his head that he was wasting his time with her? He was a good-looking kid. There were teenage girls out there who'd jump through hoops just to get his attention.

"Look, I thought we could go to the Studio tonight."

Sabrina groaned under her breath. "You're not even old enough to get through the doors." She looked distractedly past him to reassure herself that her gentleman thief was still in sight.

"There you go with that age thing again." His gaze slid away in annoyance.

She had to remind herself to be patient. After all, his grandmother had only been dead a month and he was going through a lot, although he seemed to be coping pretty well. The resilience of youth. And his youth was exactly the problem.

Taking a deep breath, she got a grip on her patience. "Right now I'm in the middle of something important and

I have to go, but you'll be hearing a lot more about this *age thing* later, my young friend." She wagged a finger in his face and disengaged her arm from his grip, then turned to look for her quarry.

Damn. He'd vanished. She'd only taken her eyes off him for a second. Except for the stalwart shopper and her trusty umbrella, the aisle was empty.

"What could be more important than an evening with me?" Behind her, Colin's voice softened persuasively.

Ignoring the question, she walked rapidly away from him, scanning the store on all sides with painstaking care. His hand closed around her arm again and forced her to stop. "Sabrina..."

She turned her head to see a coaxing grin on his face. He was growing up all right. But why couldn't he do it without causing her so much grief?

"Colin, please do me a favor and run along now. I promise we'll talk later, but I've really got to go."

He opened his mouth, but she wasn't about to stand around and argue. She turned quickly and dashed down the aisle of the accessories department, her gaze flying to the farthest reaches of the high-ceilinged old store.

If only she could have sent Colin to find security. But knowing him, he'd probably have jumped at the chance to play cops and robbers instead, and maybe get himself hurt in the process.

Judging by the way he carried himself, and the latent strength in his firm grip, that thief could be a dangerous man to cross. His sheer nerve alone was breathtaking. No, it was better to handle him herself, and hope that her wits would prove effective. That is, if she found him again.

Just when she thought she'd lost him for good, she caught sight of a familiar dark head thirty feet away and felt a tingling jolt of recognition.

He turned in her direction. She quickly darted behind a mirrored pillar, then caught sight of herself in the twin pillar across the aisle, standing out like a beacon in her scarlet linen blazer. She could see him, too. His reflection paused, and for a moment the lean, handsome face appeared to be staring right at her.

Flushed from her hiding place, she casually strolled around the counter filled with silver jewelry, keeping him in sight out of the corner of her eye. Finally she had a good view of him only one aisle away. He stood with his back to her, apparently scrutinizing another transaction.

"Okay, so you won't let me take you to a club. How about McDonald's, for a burger?"

Her breath escaped in a squeaky gasp as she put a hand to her racing heart. She'd been so intent, Colin's voice had almost made her jump out of her skin. She turned to find him at her elbow again, his fine-boned face inches from her own. Stepping back, she put a hand against his chest and gave him a determined push.

"Colin Worth, you behave yourself or I'll . . ."

"Or you'll what? Go out to dinner with me?" He grinned at her, his teeth even and white in his tanned face. Patience be damned! Right now she felt like shaking the kid till his bones rattled.

"Colin, *please.*" She craned her neck to keep the tall man in sight over his shoulder. "Look, I'll make a deal with you. Let me get back to work and I'll meet you for a Coke later, okay?"

"Do you mean that?" He gave her a suspicious look.

Sabrina grimaced. The incorrigible brat. Yes, they'd better have that little chat, and the sooner the better. But not now. Right now her attention was focused on the man moving purposefully through the Lingerie Department and on through Ladies' Shoes.

"Yes, I mean that."

"Great! Now you promised, remember." He gave her a warning look, then turned and walked away.

With a sigh of relief, she turned in the opposite direction, following her suspect as he moved down the aisle once more. The man stopped, as if undecided where to go next, and she stopped too, behind a convenient rack of scarves.

He seemed to make up his mind and his pace became more purposeful. Walking quickly, with a long, loose-limbed stride, one hand tucked elegantly in his pants pocket, he looked the essence of casual ease, for all the world like one of the male models from Worth's fashion shows. But she realized with a shock that he was taking the shortest route toward the big double doors marked No Admittance. The doors leading to the stockrooms and the back alley beyond.

After carefully lagging behind, she now broke into a near run, trying to cover the distance between them. Once again she felt panic rise up in her throat. There was no going back now. She'd have to collar him, and in the alley of all places. She could only hope and pray there'd be someone in the back room to help her, because she was going to need it.

She pushed through the heavy swinging doors just in time to see him disappear through the scratched and dented gray metal doors of the elevator. The elevator leading to the cash office.

"Oh my God!" Sprinting over to push the button, she grabbed for the black wall phone at the same time. Her fingers trembled as she punched the extension for the security office.

The money. That's what he was really after. The Brink's truck was due within the next hour for the regular

Wednesday pickup. There were two days' worth of receipts sitting in that safe upstairs. Sales were poor these days, but that still amounted to thousands of dollars.

After five interminable rings a deep male voice answered.

"Chuck, it's Sabrina," she responded breathlessly. "We've got a Code 1. He's heading for the cash office, but he also has some jewelry in his pocket. I'm on my way up." Slamming down the phone, she bit her lip and stared impatiently at the battered steel doors.

She couldn't wait for that old clunker to get back down. Pushing through the fire doors to the right of the elevator, she raced up the steps, two at a time. The ungainly clatter of her shoes on the terrazzo stairs echoed all the way up to the fifth floor. Panting for breath, she burst through the fire doors just in time to see Chuck Wilson and one of his security men escorting the tall stranger into their office.

Hovering uncertainly in the hallway, she clutched her aching side and tried to bring her breathing under control. Through the glass window of Chuck's office, she saw the security chief indicate a chair and the man sink into it with a cool smile. A smile that gave a sensuous curve to the firm, determined line of his mouth. He looked as urbane and at ease as if he owned the place.

She chewed nervously on her lower lip. Surely she didn't have to go in there? After all, she'd done her bit. There was no point in hanging around. Chuck could take it from here. Besides, she really didn't want to come face-to-face with the man. For some reason she felt embarrassed. Embarrassed...and disappointed. As if he had let her down, which was just plain stupid.

Just because he looked distinguished and prosperous didn't mean he couldn't be a thief, as well. On the contrary, that intimidating sense of power probably indicated just how successful he was at being a criminal.

Turning slowly on her heel, she pushed open the heavy fire door to the stairwell once more, doing her best to subdue the irrational feeling of disappointment. She took the stairs at a more thoughtful pace up to the seventh floor.

Seeing him pocket that jewelry had all the unreality of something that would happen in a movie. Maybe because he looked so glamorous. But unlike the movies there was nothing glamorous about crime. He was just a common thief, and he deserved everything he got.

She yanked open the door with more force than necessary and stepped into the gray carpeted hallway. Walking past the other offices, she rounded the corner into her own. Barely large enough for a desk and two tall filing cabinets, its saving grace was the window looking down on the busy traffic of King Street.

Sabrina sat down with a sigh, kicked off her loafers and wriggled her stockinged toes on the carpet. The top of her desk was covered with fabric swatches and sketches of float designs for the Santa Claus Parade, the Toronto institution that Worth's sponsored every November.

She picked up the large padded envelope lying on top. Good, the designs for the costumes had arrived. Tearing it open, she pulled out a sheaf of papers, began leafing through them, then let out a groan.

Oh, no, not more rabbits. Last year's parade was overrun with them. Turning the rabbits facedown, she sighed and looked sideways out the window, beyond the tall downtown buildings, to the cloudless July sky. Almost the exact blue of his eyes.

She expelled her breath in another sigh, impatient this time, and turned back to the desk to pick up the next design. For heaven's sake! Forget about that man and think about work—that's what she had to do.

Staring down at the page without really seeing it, she absently rubbed a finger over the tip of her nose and felt a tiny pinpoint of pain. She pulled her compact from her purse and flipped it open to examine herself in the mirror.

Her own wide, chocolate-brown eyes stared back at her, still betraying a lingering trace of disillusion, and something else she didn't want to analyze. Angling the mirror away from her disturbed expression, she turned toward the light and noticed the tiniest little scratch on the end of her nose. The diamond tiepin.

Even in that brief contact he'd left his mark on her. Whimsy gave way to a disgusted groan. Snapping the compact shut, she picked up the next design and forced herself to concentrate.

Now here was something novel—walking nutcrackers, the old-fashioned German kind straight from the Black Forest. They'd be perfect right before the Hansel and Gretel float. Penciling okay at the corner of the sheet, she moved on to the next, trying to ignore the image of that penetrating gaze that kept intruding on her thoughts. Wrinkling her brow in concentration, she slowly flipped through the sheaf, occasionally marking her approval or setting some designs aside as completely unsuitable.

The phone rang and she picked it up. "Sabrina Cates here," she replied automatically, cradling the phone on her shoulder while continuing to flip through the sketches.

"Sabrina, can you come up here? Right away? Mr. Stevenson wants to see you." Anya's normally upbeat voice sounded solemn.

She transferred the phone to the other shoulder and continued studying the sketches. "This sounds serious. Am I in the doghouse again?" Some of her ideas didn't go down well with the senior vice president. Perhaps he'd already seen the "Passion in Paradise" window.

"Don't ask me." Anya's hushed voice gave no reassurance. "I have no idea what's happening. All I know is they want to see you right now and I suggest you get up here, pronto."

"They? What could I have done so wrong that *they* would want to see me?"

"You're asking me?" Anya gave a disbelieving snort. "This from the woman whose idea of an Easter menswear window was half-naked mannequins in boxer shorts decorated with little pink bunnies!"

"Maybe Worth's isn't ready for my inspired ideas."

"That's the understatement of the century. You've come up with some of the weirdest display windows I've ever seen at Worth's."

"I thought you liked them."

"I do. I think they're great, but I don't sign your paycheck, so you'd better get up here."

"Okay, I'm on my way."

With a sigh, Sabrina put down the phone and fumbled for her shoes with her feet. With meticulous care, she checked to make sure there were no stains on her white cotton shirt and no threads clinging to her red linen trousers. If she had to walk into the lion's den, she was going to do it with confidence.

The elevator doors slid noiselessly open and she stepped out into the executive suite, her feet sinking deep into the sable carpeting. On her rare visits to the top floor she'd never been sure whether to feel in awe or oppressed by the atmosphere of hushed luxury. The carved mahogany paneling and heavy antique furniture always reminded her of a British men's club in the old movies. The kind where no one dared speak above a whisper.

The sleek receptionist gave her a curious look, then told her to go on in. Passing through a set of massive double doors, she entered the plush outer office where Anya presided as the CEO's secretary.

"Sabrina, what have you done now?" Jonathan Kent, the Display and Promotions Manager, straightened from his perch on the corner of Anya's desk and adjusted his wire-framed glasses as he gave her a quizzical look.

"You mean you don't know?"

"Not this time," he said, shaking his sandy head.

"You mean they haven't given you the gears like they usually do when I've goofed?"

"Please, don't remind me." He gave a fastidious shudder. "Now let's find out what this is all about."

Anya picked up the intercom on her desk. "Sabrina Cates is here, Mr. Stevenson." She put down the phone. Her pale green eyes widened in her freckled face as her voice dropped to an ominous whisper. "They're *all* waiting for you. You'd better go on in."

Sabrina felt the faintest touch of butterflies in her stomach. "What do you mean, *all?*"

"I mean all the VPs." Anya pushed the unruly auburn curls off her face to sink her chin on her hand and raised one ginger eyebrow in blatant curiosity.

Surely this couldn't be about something as trivial as a window design. Her mind skimmed back over the past few days. "I just can't think of anything I might have done . . . recently."

"Well, come on. The sooner we go in, the sooner we'll know. And I do have work to get back to." Grasping her elbow with firm decision, Jonathan began to lead her toward the big double doors.

He raised his hand to knock, then lowered it again and gave her a reassuring smile. "Hey, don't look so nervous. You won't be alone. I'll be there."

Sabrina smiled back, then took a deep breath as her gaze focused on the dark wood paneling carved with twining ivy leaves.

Sybil Worth's office. She could swear she caught a whiff of the heavy, flowery scent of Sybil's perfume. Impossible, of course. The family matriarch had been gone for over a month.

They had found her at her desk, slumped over her paperwork, dead at the age of seventy-eight from a massive heart attack. She had ruled Worth's for more than half a century, seeming as enduring as the granite and brick of the building itself. They called the store the Old Lady of Yonge Street, but the term had applied just as well to Sybil.

Jonathan knocked, then opened the door for her to walk through, remaining comfortingly close behind.

The first thing she noticed was Walter Stevenson and all the other vice presidents gathered at the far end of the room in one somber clump of gray flannel, almost obscuring the vast desk set before a floor-to-ceiling plate-glass window.

Sabrina faltered. Out of the corner of her mouth she murmured to Jonathan, "What is this, the Spanish Inquisition?"

"This is no time for jokes. Be serious."

He was right, but how serious could this be? After all, Colin was there, looking rather cheerful.

Through the cluster of executives, she could just see him standing behind the desk, grinning from ear to ear. In his loose-fitting white cotton shirt with the top buttons undone and the sleeves rolled up, he was a youthful contrast to the deathless conservatism of the suits around him.

The broad mischievous grin added a sparkle to his blue eyes, but rather than reassure her, it made her feel suddenly uneasy. It reminded her too vividly of the fourteen-year-old Colin she had first met, the boy who had delighted in playing pranks, like putting goldfish in the water cooler. With everyone else looking so solemn, that grin meant trouble.

But she smiled back at him for a moment, before her gaze settled once again on Walter Stevenson's heavy jowls. She advanced toward the group, dimly aware of more richly carved mahogany paneling and the beautifully ornate Victorian plaster ceiling above her head.

"Sabrina, you're wild." Colin began chuckling. "I wish I'd known what you were up to. Believe me, if I'd had any idea, there's no way you could have got rid of me."

Did that boy have no sense? She shot him a hard, meaningful look. Whatever this was all about, he wasn't helping. One glance at the rest of the unamused group told her that. And now she wasn't just mystified, she was embarrassed.

Mr. Stevenson shot Colin a reproving look over his shoulder, then turned back to her with a self-satisfied smile that made her distinctly uneasy. Whatever the old weasel had on her this time, it must be a hanging offense; nothing else would fill his beady eyes with such malicious glee.

"Miss Cates. Thank you for coming so promptly." He waved to the Queen Anne chair in front of him. "Won't you please have a seat."

Prepared to do battle, she began sinking down. The vice president stepped aside, revealing a man sitting in the high-backed leather chair behind the desk. She found herself staring directly into the cobalt-blue eyes of her gentleman thief.

Belatedly realizing that she was suspended in midair, she plunked down heavily. A quick mental check told her that her mouth wasn't hanging open like a grounded fish. Her mind raced wildly. What was he doing here? And why did the room suddenly feel hot and airless?

He sat back at ease, but studied her with the same intense scrutiny he had given the store earlier. His unwavering gaze made her mouth go dry.

To her disgust, she found herself making a mental inventory of her entire appearance, from her neatly scissored chestnut bob to the tips of her black leather loafers. Did she have a stupid look on her face? Was that the reason for the hint of a sardonic smile in the back of his eyes?

She didn't know how he'd done it. The man must be a brilliant con artist. And now the tables were turned and everyone in the room was looking at her as if *she* had done something wrong. From the imperceptible shake of his head and the expression on his face, she knew that Jonathan was even more confused.

Walter Stevenson cleared his throat. Even in her stunned state, the portentous sound irritated her.

"Miss Cates, let me introduce you to our new chief executive officer, Mr. Michael Worth."

2

SABRINA GAVE a small groan and buried her face in her hands.

"I assume that since you had him apprehended in such an embarrassing fashion, you were unaware of Mr. Worth's identity," Walter continued.

"Naturally." To her intense annoyance, the words emerged in an undignified croak.

She shot the vice president a hard look and her mouth tightened with determination. She refused to allow him to intimidate her.

But when she turned back to Michael Worth, her bravado fled before his hard, implacable gaze. It took superhuman effort to meet those deep blue eyes with their humiliating glimmer of satisfaction.

"You see, I saw you put those in your pocket...." Her gaze fell for a moment to the diamond-drop earrings shimmering on the polished desk surface between them. "Naturally I would never have...I mean I never dreamed—"

She broke off awkwardly and caught her lower lip between her teeth, then wished she hadn't when she saw his gaze drawn to her mouth. Only a brief glance, but it sent an uncomfortable wave of tingling warmth surging through her.

Walter's accusatory whine broke in on her dangerous thoughts. "Surely you knew Mr. Worth's arrival was imminent?"

Sabrina was almost grateful for the question. It gave her an excuse to transfer her attention to the vice president's scowling face. So much less disturbing than Michael Worth's relentlessly probing gaze and continuing silence. It was unnerving. It made her feel exposed and vulnerable. Why didn't he say something, for God's sake? Even if it were just to scream at her that she was an incompetent idiot and she was fired!

But his eyes only narrowed more, until the thick, silky lashes revealed only a flash of blue, making it impossible to guess his reaction to all this. "Of course I knew, Mr. Stevenson, but like everyone else I was under the impression he wasn't due till tomorrow."

She could hear the quiver in her voice and knew that silent, implacable man was intimidating her more than any person, or situation, she'd ever had to face before, and he hadn't done a thing except sit there and watch her. Watch every nuance of expression that crossed her face.

In the month since Sybil Worth's death all kinds of rumors had been circulating about the heir who ran the original Worth's in London.

Everyone knew that her only child hadn't been present at his mother's funeral. Some went so far as to blame his absence on an eighteen-year-old feud that had apparently erupted when he married against his mother's wishes. Supposedly his wife had died shortly afterward and Sybil had taken his infant son, Colin, into her care.

In her three years at Worth's she'd heard a few garbled versions of the story, but all Sabrina knew for sure was that, according to Anya, mother and son had burned up the phone and fax lines in their constant battles.

"That's no excuse for this disgraceful incident." Stevenson pressed his attack.

"It wasn't meant to be." Sabrina gave him a level look, deliberately keeping her voice low but firm. "I had no way of knowing that a man who just wandered in off the street and pocketed an expensive piece of jewelry would turn out to be Mr. Worth."

Her mouth tightening in frustration, she turned to the man behind the desk. Surely he couldn't have the same petty mind-set as Walter Stevenson. But the lean, handsome face remained inscrutable.

She was sure he could see right through her pathetic attempts at composure. The most galling part was that usually she didn't give two hoots for overbearing, power-hungry megalomaniacs. Pompous twits like Walter Stevenson could fulminate all they wanted and it rolled right off her back. But this man with his silent scrutiny had her more intimidated than she could ever remember being. She hated feeling so unequal and insecure. But she also felt an intense curiosity to know more about the black sheep son.

Officially, he hadn't made it home for Sybil's funeral because he'd been trekking in the mountains of Nepal and couldn't be reached until he returned to his base camp. By then Sybil had been dead for two weeks. But some preferred to believe that it was because he was still grieving the loss of his wife and had never forgiven his mother for refusing to accept her.

She had privately dismissed the melodramatic notion. Anya had told her that mother and son argued about more prosaic issues—such as Sybil's stubborn refusal to change with the times that had sent Worth's sales plummeting.

Having met him, Sabrina wondered for the first time if those stories could be true. But no, he was too dark and brooding and hard, without a shred of vulnerability. She couldn't imagine him pining away for anybody, and yet, what had made him so hard? Was there anything that could pierce that implacable armor?

"But how could you fail to recognize Mr. Worth?" Stevenson's voice brought her back to earth with a small jolt of self-consciousness. She had been staring at Michael Worth. Had she taken complete leave of her senses?

"I've never seen Mr. Worth before. If you don't mind my saying so, there's hardly a family resemblance."

Her gaze flickered up to the portrait hanging on the wall to her right. A society beauty in a bias-cut thirties gown. But even then, Sybil Worth's blue eyes shone with steely determination. The dynamic woman who, on her father's suicide, had rescued the store from the depression and gone on to build an empire.

Her gaze fell to Colin, who shared his grandmother's blond hair and fine-boned features. Finally her eyes came reluctantly back to meet Michael's enigmatic stare once more, to the dark, saturnine good looks.

"To be quite honest, I expected you to be a lot older, Mr. Worth."

She saw a brief flicker of surprise in his eyes.

"But you must have seen Mr. Worth's photograph in the staff newsletter," Stevenson insisted.

Sabrina barely stopped herself from rolling her eyes to heaven. The newsletter was a joke. Nobody wanted to read lectures on punctuality, or could care less about who won the executive golf day. She caught Michael Worth's steady gaze on her and flushed, praying that her reaction hadn't shown on her face.

"Obviously she didn't, Walter." There was an edge of impatience in the words Michael Worth directed to the vice president, but those hard, probing blue eyes remained fixed on her, examining her as if she were an insect on a pin. If it were anyone else, she'd take it as a kindly rescue from Walter's persecution. "How did you come to see me take those earrings, Miss Cates?"

He wasn't rescuing her from anything, but launching his own, more efficient inquisition, in a voice as even and unrevealing as his expression. But in spite of feeling so intimidated, a small shiver of awareness trickled down her spine at the sound of his husky voice, with its slight English accent that gave it such a sexy quality.

"I was following you." Someone should cut out her tongue.

"You were?" He leaned forward with quick interest. "Why?"

Now she'd gone and done it. What was she going to say? Because you're so cute?

"Yes, Miss Cates," Walter Stevenson cut in. "Why?"

And why didn't he go look for a job burning heretics at the stake?

She kept her eyes trained on Michael Worth. "You were acting in a suspicious manner. . . sir."

"Tell me, what exactly about me aroused your suspicions?"

Her palms were clammy; she surreptitiously wiped them on her knees, trying to still the faint tremor running through her body. Why did he have to be so inscrutable? Why did he have to be so good-looking? Why did he have to use the word *aroused*, and in that low, husky voice?

She licked her lips, her mouth having suddenly gone very dry. "Well, you weren't buying anything, you see. . . ."

"Surely you don't suspect every customer who doesn't buy something, Miss Cates." Stevenson spit out the accusation.

His voice was really starting to grate on her nerves, already stretched to snapping point by Michael Worth's devastating effect on her.

"But I had no idea that he . . . that you . . ."

Oh, this was too much. In horror she realized that she was near tears. Sabrina squeezed her eyes shut for a second in a desperate effort to rally her depleted defenses. She opened them to see the group of men flanking the antique rosewood desk. She'd completely forgotten their existence. But what mere mortal could ignore Michael Worth's overpowering aura of strength and command? Everyone else faded into insignificance.

"Nevertheless, it was a rather inappropriate welcome for our new CEO, don't you think?" The vice president's voice had an accusatory ring.

"Please believe me. I had absolutely no idea. I feel just dreadful about this." She turned to Jonathan for support and saw the imperceptible shake of his head.

She knew only too well what he was thinking. He'd told her so many times in the past that if she weren't so creative and talented, she'd be unemployable, given her unsurpassed knack for attracting disaster.

"And so you should," Walter Stevenson insisted.

"But I still don't understand why *you* were following me." Michael Worth cut through his vice president's bleating. "We have security personnel. Where were they?"

"I . . . I couldn't find anybody," she said in a low voice. She'd rather put up with Walter's badgering, than Michael's quiet, relentless questions. The last thing she wanted was to get Chuck into trouble.

"Pardon me, Miss Cates. Could you speak up? I couldn't hear you."

Yes he could. The bastard. He just wanted to put her on the spot. She could tell by the ruthless determination on his face. Well, she'd cowered long enough. She took a deep breath and looked him straight in the eye, saying as clearly as she could muster, "I couldn't find any security."

"So what were you planning on doing?" The question was softly put, but there was menace behind the words.

"I was going to keep you in sight, and if you left the premises . . ." Her voice trailed off. She couldn't bring herself to expose her stupidity to everyone in the room.

"Were you planning on apprehending me?" There was a slight quirk to his lips and a subtly mocking inflection in his impassive voice.

He wanted her to spell it out. He really wanted his pound of flesh, didn't he? She ground her teeth together, trying to control her mortification and hurt. Hurt? Damn it, she didn't want to feel hurt, she wanted to feel angry with his high-handed treatment.

"Did it ever occur to you that had I really been a thief and you apprehended me, I could have done you physical harm?"

"I didn't think about it at the time," she replied, stiff with resentment.

"Wasn't that a little foolhardy, Miss Cates?" His keen gaze ran over her, laced with scorn and cynicism. "You must weigh all of, what, a hundred pounds?"

"A hundred and five," she ground out, and then realized how stupid that sounded. What did five pounds signify against over six feet of well-muscled, superbly conditioned masculinity?

A hot flush crept over her skin. Angry as she was, she couldn't stop her physical reaction to him, and it made her even more furious.

"And you think you could have stopped me?" Now he was openly mocking her, with a smile that owed nothing to good humor.

What did this man want her to say? *Yes, I'm a complete nitwit!* All right, maybe it hadn't been the smartest thing to do, but for heaven's sake, she'd been protecting his store!

Seething with resentment, she could hardly choke out the words. "I was going to try."

Maybe she should be like everyone else and shrug off responsibility. This man was making her feel incredibly stupid, for doing what she thought was the right thing.

"Just hang on a minute."

The sound of Colin's voice startled her, as he pushed through the knot of men. Someone else whose existence she had forgotten until this moment.

"What did she do that was so bad?"

Suddenly, in the midst of this agonizing ordeal, she was struck by the only resemblance between father and son. They had the same eyes. The same cobalt blue. Colin's were clear and blazing now in youthful indignation.

"She put your father in a very embarrassing position, in front of the whole store." Stevenson's round face was beginning to look a little flushed.

"For Pete's sake, you act as if she did it on purpose."

"My dear Colin," he broke in, "this has nothing to do with you..."

"That's where you're wrong. If you have to blame anybody, blame me. I was there. I could have told her who he was. It's not her fault. She was just doing her job!" The boy had come up beside her and put a protective hand on her shoulder.

She saw Michael's narrowed gaze flicker to Colin's grip, then back to her. His face seemed to harden. She didn't even want to think what could be going through his mind.

"Thanks, Colin, but it was my fault. I was just too busy playing Miss Marple." She shifted nervously in her seat, trying to unobtrusively shrug off his hand.

"According to your file—" Michael leaned forward in his chair and flipped open a folder on his desk "—your *job* is Display Supervisor and you've recently been appointed coordinator of the Santa Claus Parade. Is that correct?"

His voice was cool and clipped. Once again his eyes dropped to Colin's hand on her shoulder, then back to her face, but whatever he thought, his expression gave nothing away.

"Yes." She nodded, feeling as if the ground had opened up beneath her feet.

"So therefore it is not your *job* to be trailing shoplifters around the sales floor."

"Someone has to!" Colin gripped both her shoulders and drew her protectively toward him. She strained away from the inappropriate gesture, but his fingers were like steel holding her hard against his hip.

In an agony of embarrassment, she noticed Michael's eyes narrow and his gaze shift down to her. Something dark and bleak seemed to cloud his expression for a second and another small shiver raced through her. Surely her imagination was running away with her. What did he have to be bleak about? He had it all.

Besides, he was the last man in the world she could imagine to be in need of her pity. Especially right now. If anyone needed pity, it was her. She'd always been a renegade in the staid confines of Worth's, but now she'd really done it.

Ignoring his son's outburst, Michael fixed her with a cynical look. "I'm just curious to know...why." His voice tightened. She sensed suppressed anger and couldn't understand the reason. "Why you would put yourself in that kind of jeopardy."

"Because I thought you were a thief and somebody had to stop you." Maybe it had been foolhardy, but it was the *right thing*, damn it!

"That's why we have security staff."

She let out a shaky breath of relief as his eyes slid away from her to fix Walter with a look that could have peeled paint.

She almost felt sorry for the obsequious old fool, but profoundly glad that corrosive glance wasn't aimed at her. The tone of his voice made it clear that heads would roll in that department.

Suddenly she remembered the dangerous smile on Michael's face as Chuck escorted him into the security office. She shuddered to think what he'd said to Chuck. At least the security chief could console himself that *her* head was now on the chopping block, too. In the long line of incidents that punctuated her career at Worth's, this had to be *the* most disastrous.

"However, Colin, you're quite right." Michael gave his son a long considering look. Colin's fingers tightened painfully on her shoulders. As casually as possible, she reached up and nudged his hands away. Michael's impenetrable gaze dropped to meet hers and held it for what seemed like an eternity. Then he continued. "Miss Cates was just doing her job."

She let out an incredulous breath of relief, even as her anger came to a boil again. If he felt that way, why did he put her through the third degree? Just to see her squirm?

"You're damn right," Colin broke in. "And a very good job she does, too, for your information."

Sabrina glanced up at him, distracted for a moment from her self-righteous indignation by Colin's uncharacteristic aggression and rudeness. She darted a look at Michael, holding her breath for his reaction.

But the granite mask betrayed no response to his son's outburst. He turned his gaze on her, pinning her to the spot. "I'd like to think that each and *every* person working in this store would do the same thing you did. But I have no right to expect that level of loyalty. Your personal safety, Miss Cates, means far more to us than a pair of diamond earrings."

His words were formal and sincere, but with a trace of irony that told her he wasn't so much impressed by her heroism as he was marveling at her stupidity.

"Thank you, Mr. Worth. That's gratifying to know." She lifted her chin and looked him in the eye, letting a hint of sarcasm edge into her voice. Whatever he thought of her actions, she wouldn't be cowed.

Something dark and dangerous flared deep in his eyes and a small smile curved his lips, setting off a strange fluttering deep inside her. Abruptly she dropped her gaze to stare at her hands clutched tightly in her lap.

She must be more stressed-out than she had thought. For those few seconds something disturbing had passed between them, some kind of magnetic force pulling her inexorably to him. As if he had the power to bend her to his will.

For a moment it frightened her. And the acute awareness was only intensified by the sudden heavy silence that had fallen in the room.

Then Walter Stevenson cleared his throat and she was never so glad of anything than the sound of his fawning pronouncement. "Well, now, after all, Miss Cates, Mr. Worth needs to see for himself how we operate around here." He put his hands behind him and rocked back on his heels in smug self-importance.

She shot him a sideways glance and tightened her lips. The old toad must have picket holes in his rear end from sitting on so many fences.

"Perhaps this demonstration was a trifle drastic, however." He forced a dry chuckle and the white-haired suits around him joined in a wave of condescending laughter.

Sabrina managed a faint smile.

"On the contrary, that's exactly what I do want to see," Michael Worth cut in, shooting her an arch look. "Within reason, that people do their best for the store all the time, not just when they think they're being watched."

She felt the hot flush rise to her cheeks. He'd done nothing but *watch* her from the moment she walked into the room. It had been the most unnerving experience in all her twenty-seven years.

Now he closed her file with a decisiveness that told her the interview was over. "You'll find a token of our appreciation in your next paycheck. That will be all, Miss Cates."

Her head was spinning and she felt as limp as a rag doll after the roller-coaster ride her emotions had taken. She rose to her feet, bracing herself against the arms of the chair, determined to gather her wits and leave the new CEO with a more favorable impression.

"Thank you very much." It took superhuman effort to stop her hand from trembling as she thrust it toward him. "And I'd like to take this opportunity to welcome you to Worth's." It was about time she started acting like the professional, capable woman that she was.

There was a small titter of disapproval around her. No doubt she'd committed a gross breach of protocol, but she might as well be hung for a sheep as a lamb.

After an infinitesimal hesitation, he slowly got to his feet and took her hand in his, wrapping his warm fingers around her cold ones in a firm grip.

"Thank you." He inclined his head slightly, still grave, but there was a quiver at the corner of his mouth. Could he possibly be fighting back something as human as a genuine smile?

His keen gaze and the feeling of his firm, warm fingers were doing strange things to her pulse. She withdrew her hand and shoved it into the pocket of her jacket as she turned away, swallowing her heart.

So much for her resolution to stay strictly professional. Boy, was she a sap. But then again, when it came right down to it, she couldn't ignore what had attracted her in the first place. He was the handsomest man she'd ever seen. Let's face it, she'd have to be dead not to be affected. Any woman would.

In a vague sort of way she'd wondered what Sybil's son would be like, but today had blown any banal preconceptions to smithereens. He was dark, secretive, fascinating and much too dangerous to her peace of mind.

"Feel like grabbing that Coke now?" Colin murmured as he dropped into step beside her. "I bet you need one after all that. I know I do." They had reached the door and he was about to open it for her, but his father's quiet voice stopped him.

"I'm afraid you'll have to take a rain check. There's business to attend to. I'm sure Miss Cates understands."

She heard Colin suck in his breath with a sharp hiss and looked up to see a dull red flush darken his tanned cheeks. His lips compressed into a straight, obstinate line.

"Can't you wait till I've had a break?" He turned to face his father with an insolence that shocked her. This wasn't like Colin at all.

In the sudden deathly silence, she could hear the soft sounds of feet scuffing on the carpet as people shifted nervously.

"I can wait, but I wouldn't expect everyone else to. Would you?"

A small tremor raced through her at that warm, black velvet voice behind her. Michael sounded reasonable and very calm, but a quick glance over her shoulder showed her the determination in his face.

Colin gave her a tight smile and stepped away from the door to let her pass. The large office had gone very still and the air vibrated with an electric tension that was almost tangible. Practically lunging for the door, she whipped it open and made her escape.

MICHAEL WATCHED the young woman leave the room. She was unlike anyone he'd ever come across before. He fought back a smile, remembering her groan of horror when she first saw him.

People didn't usually display their emotions in such a dramatic fashion. Nobody *he* knew, and certainly not in a business meeting.

He looked around at the sober, disapproving faces ranged on either side. They really had it in for poor Sabrina Cates. Walter had spent most of the time before she arrived complaining that the girl was a menace and lamenting how difficult it was to fire people these days.

Didn't he know it. A lot of changes were desperately needed at Worth's; he'd known that for years. But it was too bad that he had to wait until Sybil died to set things right. He could only pray it wasn't too late.

Walter and the rest of the old guard were dead set against change of any kind. It was long past time they retired, but for once he couldn't bring himself to force the issue. He'd known most of these men since his childhood.

After all those years Walter had spent ingratiating himself with Sybil in order to reach the senior vice presidency, he now seemed to be enjoying every pompous moment of it. His smug attitude at Sabrina's discomfort had been unforgivable. And with the store in its present disastrous financial straits, Walter should know better than to waste his time with this ridiculous vendetta.

But he could understand why Sabrina Cates got under Walter's skin. Now he understood the source of Walter's frustrated tirade about "that girl." She hadn't been one bit intimidated or impressed by the vice president's overbearing manner.

And when she turned her unwavering look on him, when he looked into those fathomless coffee-colored eyes, he himself had felt extremely disconcerted, to say the least.

According to her file she was twenty-seven, but she looked much younger. Maybe it was the way her glossy chestnut hair framed her face in a short, unpretentious bob. Over and over again, he'd found his gaze drawn to the fullness of her mouth, painted that deep, dramatic crimson. It was a dangerous compulsion, and he knew he should stop, but he hadn't been able to keep his eyes off the slight pout of her lower lip that made her mouth look...

And her skin... It was amazing, so creamy, so translucent, so soft that he was blown away by the unexpected urge to reach out and brush his fingertips over her cheek.

Even now the thought made him shift uncomfortably in his chair. At the time he'd been absolutely mortified and wondered where the hell that thought had come from. He just prayed she hadn't been able to see any of that in his face.

But he was very much afraid that she'd noticed. He'd heard something in her voice, that husky voice so unexpectedly deep for someone so small.

An acute wave of embarrassment swept over him all over again and he felt a dull heat in his face. He couldn't believe he'd been so crude. God forbid he was deteriorating into one of those disgusting men who preyed on their female employees.

"So what was so important, you couldn't wait?" His son's petulant voice brought him back abruptly to his surroundings.

They were all still there, looking at him, waiting for him. And suddenly he found himself wishing they'd all just disappear. Wishing he were someone else. Someone who could get up and follow Sabrina Cates to wherever she was going.

"That will be all, gentleman. Thank you." The dismissed vice presidents filed out. With a reluctance he abhorred as cowardice, he turned to his son. Only to be faced with the usual belligerent stance. "Take a seat, Colin. We have a few things to discuss."

The boy sank down into the chair with ill-concealed resentment.

A frown creased his brow. His son appeared to be smitten with puppy love. He knew it had to happen eventually, but it took him by surprise. Sometimes he had to remind himself that Colin was no longer a little boy. He was growing up, experiencing all those normal urges.

It wasn't hard to see why he'd be attracted to Sabrina Cates, but she was too old for Colin.

So what was he thinking, that she was just right for him? He was disgusted with himself for thinking that way, and even more disgusted that he had virtually ogled her.

It was still embarrassing to think how his gaze had run over her small, slender figure. Even now he could see the image of her sitting in the very chair Colin now occupied, and through her shirt the faintest shadow of lace had been visible, curving over the swell of her breast. He'd torn his gaze away, shocked at what he was doing, only to find her dark, intent eyes watching him.

Once again he squirmed with embarrassment. It was a salutary reminder. Better stick to business. Good business and proper ethics demanded that he not get involved with his female employees. Not even think about them in that way. Besides, he had enough problems. Most important of all, his son.

"So what's all this nonsense I hear about backpacking around Europe, Colin?"

AFTER QUICKLY TIDYING her desk, Sabrina shoved the costume designs in her briefcase, then raced for the elevator, late for her date. Charlie would understand. Who could blame her for being a little distracted? It wasn't every day you got your new boss practically arrested. That was quite a feat, even for her.

Reaching the main sales floor, she hurried toward the doors leading out onto Yonge Street, then came to a skidding stop. Turning to her right, she dashed over to the perfume counter.

The woman behind the counter smiled. "Hi, Sabrina. What'll it be this evening?"

"You tell me, Doris. I'm meeting Charlie."

"Hmm... How about this? It's light and summery and just a bit old-fashioned." She held out a delicate crystal flacon of pale gold L'Air du Temps.

With a smile, Sabrina took the bottle and liberally sprayed her wrists and throat before aiming a quick spray behind her ear.

Doris gasped, staring in shock over Sabrina's shoulder. She turned slowly to find Michael Worth standing behind her, looking down at an ugly wet patch on the lapel of his immaculate navy suit.

"Oh, Mr. Worth." This *couldn't* be happening to her. "I'm so sorry." She glanced back at the salesclerk in panic and saw that Doris had brought out a box of tissues and was holding a cluster toward her. "Here, please allow me..."

Taking the tissues with one hand, she splayed the other across his chest, then began dabbing ineffectually at the spot on his lapel, trying to soak up the perfume that had already seeped into the fine wool, and leaving tiny little flecks of tissue behind.

If she'd only been concentrating she would have realized that her efforts were not only futile, they were making things worse. Now instead of a wet spot that would have eventually evaporated, he had an ugly patch of lint marring the perfection of his lapel. But all she could think of was how warm and solid he felt, his heart beating slow and steady beneath the suit and crisp white shirt.

He stopped her with a firm grip on her wrist and she stared at his hand holding hers. Although well manicured, it wasn't the soft, pampered hand she might have expected. She could feel the callused ridge of his palm and see that the tips of his long, lean fingers were callused, too. Such a strong, masculine hand.

Slowly she lifted her gaze to meet a long, glittering intense look. Then, without warning, he smiled, and she was stunned by the transformation. That grim intensity vanished, to be replaced by a flash of white teeth and eyes that crinkled at the corners with a lazy sensuality that had her knees turning to jelly. If that wasn't bad enough, a rakish dimple appeared in his left cheek.

What a tantalizing contrast to that cool, formal executive demeanor. This was a test—she knew it—sent by a malevolent fate to torture her already overstressed libido.

It was hard to believe this was the same formidable man who had so disconcerted her this afternoon. But maybe not. Deep in his eyes she could still discern that impenetrable wall shielding the private Michael Worth from the world.

"Thank you." He coolly took the tissues from her hand. "It's quite all right. I can manage. Please, continue with your pilfering."

She choked on a gasp and began to cough, then recovered herself sufficiently to say, "I don't blame you for being ticked off."

A brief curve of the lips momentarily softened the hard lines of his face. "But I'm not . . . ticked off." The expression sounded so stilted and strange on his lips, and said in that grave formal manner it made her smile involuntarily. "Consider it recompense for the injury done to you."

And then before she knew what he meant to do, he placed his index finger gently, and briefly, on the tip of her nose. "I hope you've recovered from our collision."

He remembered. "It . . . it was nothing," she stammered, taken aback by the incredible surge of electricity racing through her at his gossamer touch.

"Good. . .good." He seemed to collect himself and gave her a more restrained smile. "You smell very nice, and thanks to you so will I, at the business dinner I'm attending."

"Oh, no . . ." She put her hands to her burning cheeks. "I'm sorry."

"I don't mind. But next time, perhaps you could choose a fragrance that's a little more—" he sniffed his lapel "—me."

Like what? Eau de gorgeous?

With a slight nod and a murmured good-night, he walked away toward the main doors.

"Did I hear you say Mr. Worth?"

Doris's voice brought her abruptly out of her stupor. She tore her eyes away from his tall, athletic frame and turned to face the other woman.

"Uh-huh. That's our new boss."

"Pretty cool customer."

She nodded in agreement with Doris. But there was absolutely nothing cool about the way he made her feel. For a moment she was overcome with a premonition of disaster, but she shook it off. She was just overreacting to a simple physical attraction. A disastrously inappropriate one, perhaps, but nothing to justify this insidious sense of danger. She determinedly pushed it from her thoughts and headed for the revolving doors.

Emerging onto the sidewalk, she looked up to see Michael Worth about to get into a long black limousine pulled up at the curb.

He glanced at her and broke into a wry smile. "Can I offer you a lift?"

"Oh . . . thank you," she said in surprise, "but that's not necessary. I haven't far to go." She waved an arm in the direction of the restaurant across the street.

"In that case, I'll say good-night." He smiled and climbed in as the uniformed chauffeur held the door open.

In the dim interior, she noticed a pair of long, elegant legs clad in sheer black hose and delicate, expensive evening pumps. The legs moved over to let Michael in and Sabrina's smile faded.

The driver shot her a sidelong, curious glance. She spun on her heel and walked off quickly as the limo pulled away.

Shame on her. The hired help, daring to lust after Michael Worth. She paused in the doorway of the crowded restaurant, then spotted Charlie's snow-white head and hurried over to the table beside the large window that looked out on the bustle of Yonge Street.

"I'm so sorry I'm late."

A smile wreathed his lined face when he saw her. He slowly rose to his feet and came around to hold out her chair. He was a gentleman of the old school, and she loved him for it. In spite of their age difference, he was her best friend.

When she first came to Worth's three years ago, fresh out of school and knowing no one, they'd thrown her in at the deep end, not just doing displays, but putting her in charge of Santa's Castle in the toy department, smack-dab in the middle of the pre-Christmas madhouse.

That first day Charlie had watched from his red velvet throne as she dashed around, pretending that she could easily cope with the zoo. He'd quickly seen the uncertainty beneath her bravado. As soon as he found out she was alone in Toronto, far from home and family, he'd become a kind of surrogate father and friend.

By the end of that Christmas season, he *was* Santa Claus to her. The gift he gave was confidence in herself, helping her to see that she didn't have to be afraid of the competitive, demanding job she'd taken on.

As she sank down in her seat, Charlie sniffed appreciatively. "Stopped by the perfume counter on your way out again, didn't you?" His warm gray eyes crinkled at the corners as he smiled.

"Yes, and don't I wish I hadn't." Sabrina went on to tell him about the most recent disaster and then what had happened earlier in the day.

Charlie laughed and laughed. By the time she had got through all the demoralizing details, he was dabbing at the tears with the corner of his napkin.

Finally his laughter died away and he shook his head. "Well, now. Don't let it worry you too much. Mr. Worth sounds like a reasonable kind of man."

Sabrina gave him a small smile and gazed out of the window at the crowds of commuters heading for the subway in the pleasant summer evening. *Reasonable* sounded so wishy-washy when applied to someone as vital and dominating as Michael Worth. He impressed her as a man who had the power to shape the world exactly as he wished.

"But, you know, what bothered me most, Charlie, was Colin's rudeness. I've never seen him behave that way before."

"I have. Don't forget I've known that boy since he was knee-high to a grasshopper. He's basically a good kid, until he doesn't get his own way."

She sighed. "You're right. I like Colin, but it's a shame he's been so spoiled. You have to admit though, he could have been a real brat. As it is, he's pretty likable."

"Who wouldn't be likable, when their every whim is indulged? And we all know his grandmother doted on him," Charlie said knowingly. "But from what you've told me, I have a feeling things will be different now that his father is here."

"Yes, but...how different? I'm afraid things might take a turn for the worse. Colin really resents his father."

"That's natural for a teenager. They're always rebellious. He'll grow out of it."

"I guess so." But she wasn't convinced. "I couldn't imagine speaking to my parents the way Colin spoke to his father today."

She thought of the mixture of tolerance, good-humored discipline and occasional exasperation that marked her father's dealings with herself and her three teenage brothers.

"You can't compare their relationship to the one you grew up with. Don't forget, the boy has always lived with his grandmother while his father lived in England."

"I guess you're right. Colin's never really talked much about his family, even though I was kind of like a big sister to him . . . until recently," she added gloomily.

"Is he still bothering you with that?" Charlie smiled with understanding.

"Yes, but I plan on nipping it in the bud, once and for all."

While they waited for their order she sank her chin on her fist and stared out the window, recalling Michael's face, his intense blue eyes, that smile that acted on her like a potent drug.

Where had he been going? A business dinner like he said or . . . She couldn't help wondering who the woman could be. Probably some pampered socialite who had never done anything distasteful, like work, in her life. But she shouldn't be catty. It was only natural he'd be with someone like that.

"So why don't you tell me about that young man?"

She gave a guilty start and turned to Charlie. "What young man?"

"The handsome one you were talking to," he said casually while he buttered his roll.

"That was Michael Worth."

"Oh, I see." Charlie gave her a keen, piercing look.

"You know, he's a very intense, powerful man," she murmured abstractedly.

"Oh, really?"

She looked over to see his head tipped to one side and a knowing gleam in his gray eyes.

"Oh, Charlie... You're on the wrong track." She laughed, embarrassed to be so transparent. "He's Michael Worth."

"So? He's also a man."

"Oh, no. No, that's impossible. And you can stop matchmaking."

She saw the warmth in his eyes, the love and affection.

"Sabrina, I was deliriously happy with my darling Amy. We had over fifty years together. Can you blame me if I want to see you that happy, too?"

With a sigh, she took his wrinkled hand in hers. Gazing down at the long slender fingers, a mist of sudden tears obscured her vision.

Charlie gave her hand a squeeze. "Why the tears, you kid with the face?" He teased her gently, his eyes twinkling with a smile again.

She laughed at the funny endearment reserved especially for her and wiped at her cheeks. "It must have been so easy for Amy to fall in love with you. You probably swept her off her feet with your smile."

Even now, in his seventies, he was very handsome, and carried his tall, portly frame with an upright bearing enhanced by a trim white mustache.

"As a matter of fact, I did, but is that any reason to cry?"

She laughed at his dry tone. "I'm lucky to have you as a friend, Charlie." She lifted his hand to her lips and kissed it.

"It's not right." His gentle voice became serious and his gray eyes earnest. "You should be concentrating on getting yourself a young man."

"How does one go about *getting* a man?" she teased. "Should I grease up the old shotgun?" At Charlie's grimace, she went on. "Good men are hard to find. And I don't have time to go out hunting."

He refused to see the joke. "Maybe you'd have better luck if you spent less time with an old guy like me."

But she just smiled and leaned across the table to kiss the tip of his nose. "If I could find someone half as handsome and gallant as you are, Charlie, I'd snap him up in a minute."

Without bidding, Michael Worth's blue eyes came to mind. *Yeah, and pigs can fly.*

3

SABRINA GROANED and sank down onto the carpet beside her desk. Careful not to disturb the long string of float illustrations laid out along the floor, she slowly straightened her cramped legs in front of her and lowered her aching back to the carpet. Hunching over the designs all day was murder on the muscles.

With her arms flung above her head, she stretched with all her might. The full skirt of the blue cotton dress billowed around her as she drew her knees up to lengthen her spine, then swayed them back and forth in time to the song on the radio. It was a quiet afternoon. As long as the door was closed, nobody would complain. Besides, the music helped her to think.

She started singing along with Rod Stewart. The door swung open and she stopped with a gasp. "Mr. Worth!"

Frozen to the spot, she found herself noticing every tiny detail with crazy, almost detached, precision. How blue his eyes looked as they stared down at her in shock, their brilliance accentuated by the jewel-colored paisley tie, such a dramatic contrast to the sober charcoal pin-striped suit.

Stunned by the sudden surge of heat rushing to his loins, Michael sucked in his breath, trying to suppress the carnal response of his body. Sabrina lay on the carpet, arms flung wide, her knees drawn up and the full skirt of her dress fallen back to reveal long, slender thighs.

"Yes, I did knock." For once his expression was very easy for Sabrina to read. He was appalled.

His dry voice betrayed nothing, but she saw his eyes sliding down the length of her legs in thorough appraisal, taking in every inch of exposed thigh.

The scorching flush started at her toes and raced up to her face as Sabrina scrambled to her feet among the scattered papers, wishing the floor would just open up and swallow her. Who could blame him now if he had serious doubts about her professionalism?

When Rod Stewart's suggestive growl filled the silence, she practically tripped over her feet, darting over to switch off the radio.

"There's no need to turn your music off on my account." Exuding strength and vitality, Michael Worth took up all the space in her tiny little room with his overpowering presence.

"That's all right. I was just, um—you're probably wondering what I was doing down there," she finished in a desperate rush.

"Organizing your files?" She heard the tinge of mockery in his low voice, saw it in his eyes.

All she could do was stare up at him, prey once again to that dangerous sexual fascination. Any normal man would show some kind of response to her flagrant exposure. She might not be a raving beauty, but she wasn't exactly repulsive, either. Yet after that thorough appraisal, he betrayed not the slightest hint of reaction. Clearly, she left him cold.

She should be glad. She didn't want him to feel any other way but, damn it, her vanity was wounded. But this was absolutely the worst time to dwell on her offended pride.

"No, I organized my files yesterday. I knew you'd make your way over here sooner or later."

"Oh? How did you know that?" His expression hardened with a hint of suspicion.

"Well, you've checked out all the other departments." How stupid did he think she was? He'd been working his way methodically through the store. Then again, from what he'd seen so far, she couldn't blame him if he thought she was clueless.

"I see." The words were clipped and businesslike, a touch dismissive, his lean, impassive face even more grave than usual as he glanced down at the papers on the floor. "If I've caught you at a bad time I can come back."

But she knew that was mere politeness. His time was too valuable to waste on small talk, or on coming back at the convenience of a lowly employee.

"No, no. Just give me a second and I'll clear those papers out of your way."

Eyes glittering between thick lashes, his gaze dropped slowly to her feet. She followed the look until she saw her own stocking-clad toes and quickly sidled behind the desk. It just went from bad to worse.

Groping under the desk with one outstretched foot, she laughed weakly and began a desperate search. "Those shoes were here a minute ago."

So much for making a good impression. Where on earth were those shoes?

"Perhaps I can be of assistance."

Before she knew what he meant, he stepped in and shut the door behind him with a quiet click. Adroitly picking his way through the papers on the floor, he dropped the fat folder he was carrying onto the crowded desktop, then came around to her, an ironic expression on his face.

"Please, allow me." He gestured toward her chair with a smile and she flopped down in bewilderment. And then he was down on his knees in front of her, bending to retrieve her shoes.

"Oh, no!" Now she saw what he intended. "Really, I can manage!"

But he just gave her a solemn smile and held out one black patent pump. With as much aplomb as she could muster in her embarrassed state, she slipped in her foot. But at the accidental brush of his fingers on her ankle, an electric current went zinging up her leg, a river of tingling heat that spread through her with shocking, erotic effect.

Stunned, Sabrina could only stare down at his head bent over her knees as he reached for her other shoe. She should jump up and tell him to stop. She should tell him she could manage. She shouldn't just sit here, transfixed, staring at his thick, silky hair, desperately fighting the urge to reach forward, slide her fingers through the strands, pull him closer and kiss his lips off. Her cheeks burned as she desperately tried to wipe all kinds of forbidden fantasies from her mind. He was dangerously perceptive.

Then he rocked back on his heels to look up at her. Still so impassive, so grave, but the subtle light flaring in the back of his eyes hinted that he wasn't impassive at all. The man was virtually impossible to read, and maybe she was just being fanciful, imagining he could be affected anywhere near as acutely as her.

"How's that?"

"That's just fine, thank you." She tried so hard to be nonchalant, but her voice came out in an undignified gasp.

Breathless at his closeness, she couldn't tear her eyes away from his face, from the firm, straight lips, from the lock of dark hair that persisted in falling onto his brow, slightly furrowed now, giving his gaze that intent directness that wreaked such havoc on her composure. Her cheeks burned even hotter. Her fascination with him must be written all over her face.

"Now perhaps we can get down to business."

The words jolted her out of the fantasy. There was nothing of Prince Charming in his actions. He had just wanted to cut through her dithering and save his precious time.

As he began to rise, she jumped to her feet. "I'll just clear..."

Her head hit the underside of his jaw with a hollow crunch. She heard his teeth snap together and a yelp of pain.

"...the chair," she finished with a wince, reaching up to massage the aching spot on her scalp.

Only inches away, he stood over her with one hand clasped over his chin, his face distorted with pain, a thunderous look darkening his eyes. "Miss Cates." The words had an odd inflection as if he were holding his breath, probably trying hard to control the urge to strangle her.

"Yes, Mr. Worth," she answered in a small voice, her eyes wide as she stared up at him.

He glared at her for a moment. "Just sit down." He backed away, never taking his eyes from hers. "It's safer that way."

To her horror, she erupted in a burst of laughter. It had to be nerves—either that or she was losing her wits. Michael raised a questioning eyebrow that instantly sobered her.

"Do you realize how ludicrous we must look," she explained, "clutching our sore spots and eyeing each other as if we were about to explode?"

"Unfortunately I do."

The wry comment was a sharp reminder that he'd come to her office on business. What was she doing, wasting his time with this foolishness?

"Won't you please sit down." With stiff formality, she slowly took her seat and folded her hands on the desk.

Michael lowered his tall, lean body into the battered oak chair opposite.

She cleared her throat. "Well . . . what can I do to you—I mean, for you?"

"I think you've done everything to me you possibly could." A brief, derisive smile curved his mouth.

"Not quite everything." Involuntarily her gaze traveled the length of his body; then she saw that he had caught her looking.

Her face flamed in disgust. She might as well take out a full-page ad in the *Toronto Star*. Sabrina Cates makes a big fat fool of herself over Michael Worth!

But there was only irony in his expression. "Thanks for the warning."

She had to get a grip on herself. This man didn't miss a thing. And all she could offer was a halfhearted explanation. "These things just keep happening."

"Like what kind of things?"

Now there really was amusement in his soft, husky voice and it didn't slow down her accelerating heartbeat one little bit.

"Oh, you don't want to know. And I'm too embarrassed to say." She laughed awkwardly, trying to relieve the tension building up inside.

He flipped open the bulging folder in front of him on the desk and quickly scanned the contents. "You mean, like the time Mr. Rumpy and Miss Flowerpot got into a fist-fight during their show in the children's department?"

She gaped at him in surprise, glanced at the folder and began to laugh. He raised a quizzical eyebrow.

"I'm sorry." She shook her head. "It's just that those names sound so funny coming from you."

His only answer was to raise the eyebrow even higher.

Fighting to subdue her amusement, she caught her bottom lip between her teeth in the effort to stop it from quivering. But the irrepressible grin spread as she went on, "Apparently, Mr. Rumpy was cheating on Miss Flowerpot and she found out just before the show began. How could I possibly have known when I hired them that she'd slug him right in the middle of 'On the Good Ship Lollipop'?"

He didn't seem to share her humor; then again, not many people at Worth's did.

"Sounds like Mr. Rumpy got what he deserved," he said dryly.

"He certainly did. And the kids thought it was the best show they'd seen in a long time, the bloodthirsty little devils." She smiled.

"The parents weren't happy. We got quite a few outraged letters, I believe."

Sabrina shook her head. "Isn't it funny how sometimes when people become parents they completely lose their sense of humor."

After a long considering look, he answered gravely, "Maybe they don't have much of a sense of humor to begin with."

"In that case they might as well be dead."

His gaze ran over her, unsmiling. "You can't always laugh your way through life."

"You can't take it that seriously, either."

"Some things have to be taken seriously. If I went around laughing all day, my board of directors would have me committed."

"Yes, I'm afraid they would." Somehow this conversation had got away from her. She had the feeling they weren't discussing those other parents anymore.

"Don't you ever take anything seriously?"

His question took her aback, but she replied quickly, "Of course I do. I'm very serious about my job."

"I'm glad to hear it." Before he started breaking down and asking her to rescue him, he'd better get back to the business that had brought him here. The trouble was that, whenever she was around, business seemed to flee from his mind.

"Although I know Walter Stevenson thinks I'm a menace."

A small grim smile curved his mouth. "True, but you must admit some of your ideas have backfired spectacularly."

She nodded with regret. "I don't think he's ever forgiven me for that boa constrictor."

"You can rest assured of that. He made quite a point of that incident." Michael tapped a finger on the sheaf of papers in front of him.

"What is that... enormous folder you have there?"

"It's your employee record. Walter personally compiled it with exhaustive thoroughness."

She sank her head to her hands. "Oh, no." Then she looked up. "It's... rather large, isn't it?"

He riffled through the densely written pages. "It certainly is... and damned heavy to carry around."

Obviously, Walter hadn't missed anything. Did he keep track of her visits to the bathroom, too? Mind you, she'd managed to make things ten times worse in the brief period since meeting Michael. She had no defense.

Then suddenly he slapped the folder closed, picked it up and dumped it in the wastebasket, where it landed with a satisfying thunk.

Sabrina could only gape in shock.

"However, accidents aside, I value creative enthusiasm and you seem to have it in abundance. It's exactly what this store needs to survive."

"Thank you." She was still stunned. What was Walter going to say?

"You're welcome." He had to wrench his gaze away, trying to ignore the way the blue fabric of her dress clung and stretched across her small, rounded breasts. "I believe the grapevine around here is remarkably efficient. You probably know by now there'll be extensive changes happening in the near future." Back on familiar ground he felt more in control.

What was the matter with him? Had he lost his wits? He'd been his own master for too long to fall prey to this kind of immature, schoolboy behavior. But that was just it—he wasn't being himself. He'd gone through a lot in the past month, true, but that was no excuse.

"I had heard something of the sort," she murmured, but she was distracted by his movement as he leaned back in the chair and his jacket fell open. For a moment she allowed her gaze to dwell on his broad, firm chest, lovingly molded by the snowy white shirt.

"I want to refocus the company image, starting by renovating the physical appearance of the store." He pinned her with a direct blue gaze. "Now you're probably wondering what all this has to do with you...."

No, she was wondering what it would it be like to feel his firm, sensuous lips on hers. Would they be hard and demanding, or soft and persuasive? Cool like a sip of sparkling wine, or warm and ardent. She was obsessed, that was it. Obsessed by this man, and it was completely silly.

"I believe you've had some...difficulty getting your ideas across."

Taking a deep breath, she tried to rein in her galloping heartbeat. "They've been flatly turned down, actually."

"I spoke to Jonathan Kent. He had a lot of nice things to say about you."

"He did?" She met his speculative look and felt her pulse quicken again. Sitting up a little straighter, she made a determined effort to pull herself together. She must be nuts, finding a conversation like this sexy.

"Jonathan showed me some of the proposals he'd had to veto because they were too radical for Worth's. He thought they were brilliantly creative, and I agree. He says your talents are wasted in such a conservative environment. I agree with that, too. But we're selfish enough to want to keep you here."

For the first time in her life she was actually speechless. "Thank you," she managed to say at last.

There was something so heartfelt about her reaction, it took him aback a little, and at the same time gave him an absurd sense of pleasure. It was foolhardy to feel this way about what was, after all, just a good business decision. But then, his feelings had nothing to do with the businessman in him.

The last time he'd felt like this he'd been eighteen years old. My God, was this his midlife crisis already? Was he dwindling into some pathetic old character, grasping after his lost youth in this vibrant, alive young woman? *Stick to business, Michael, before you make a mess of things.*

He took a deep breath and sat a little more upright in the chair, trying to focus on the matter at hand. "I need some ideas. The store needs a breath of fresh air, a whole new approach to display that will help build an image we can associate with the new Worth's. From now on, I want you to bring your ideas directly to me."

Resting his long, tapered fingers on the battered oak surface of her desk, he leaned slightly toward her. With a small quiver, she remembered the latent strength of those warm fingers.

"You mean I don't have to run the gamut of old Stonewall Stevenson and the bedpan brigade—" She stopped abruptly, realizing what she'd said and who she'd said it to. But she looked up to find only an ironic glitter in his narrowed eyes. "I beg your pardon. I..."

He held up a hand to stop her. "Everyone's entitled to their opinion." A sly smile quirked one corner of his mouth and that delectable dimple appeared to torment her. "I can only say that Walter is equally unflattering where you are concerned."

She grinned. "Fair enough." Once again she'd opened her big mouth and put her foot in it, but Michael Worth was too much of a gentleman to make an issue out of it.

"I'm also interested in seeing your files on the parade. Please have them sent up to my office."

He rose to his feet, and she did the same, feeling dwarfed by his height and his sheer physical presence in the confined space.

With a quiet smile, she held out her hand across the desk. "Thank you, Mr. Worth, for this wonderful opportunity. You won't be disappointed."

He took her hand and she suddenly felt shy and very small as his warm fingers closed around hers.

"I'm sure I won't be, Miss Cates. In matters of business I'm seldom wrong. I only hope your ideas are as creative as your turn of phrase." Michael inclined his head toward her in a brief, jerky acknowledgment and gave her a searching look.

He was still holding her hand. She slowly dropped her gaze to their clasped hands, then back up to his face again. As if in sudden realization, he let go of her fingers, his manner brisk and businesslike once more.

"I'll let you get back to . . . whatever it is you were doing on the floor." Mocking amusement glimmered in the back of his eyes.

He started for the door and she darted around the desk to open it for him. As he walked past, his eyes briefly held hers; then she closed the door behind him. She sagged against the frosted glass and let out a huge breath.

Once again the memory flashed through her mind—the feel of him, hard and warm beneath his suit, the way her hand had molded to the contours of his chest. Just thinking about it made her knees shake.

Enough.

She'd always had a pretty philosophical approach to life and relationships. One day you turned a corner, met someone and something clicked. That didn't mean it had to work out.

After all, her previous relationships hadn't. Granted, there were only two involvements she could call serious—one in college and one just after she joined Worth's. Both guys were nice, but there had been no *magic.* She hadn't felt whatever that feeling was that meant this was the man she wanted to spend her life with.

Both relationships had dissolved by mutual consent and they'd gone their separate ways with no broken hearts. And right now she wasn't looking. She didn't believe in going out and hunting for love. That was desperation and she wasn't desperate. She was happy with her life.

If something was meant to be, then it would happen. But this time fate had really let her down. She *couldn't* feel this way about Michael. The CEO of Worth's was absolutely out of her league.

Fate might dish out the choices, but it was up to her to make the best of them, and she prided herself on being too smart to make such a basic mistake.

Then she remembered the reason for his visit and gave a little hop of glee, bebopping along to her desk, snapping her fingers and humming tunelessly. Finally she could let her imagination take flight! Fate had handed her this, too, and never in her wildest dreams had she expected an opportunity like this. And at Worth's, of all places!

Now she finally had a real challenge. She wanted to prove herself. She wanted to dazzle him.

But impressing Michael Worth meant more than pandering to her libido. She didn't want to end her life doing display windows. This could be the perfect stepping stone into the in-house marketing and advertising department where she could find real scope for her creativity. And after Worth's, who knew? The sky was the limit.

MICHAEL PUNCHED the elevator button marked Up and shoved his hands in his trouser pockets, disturbed and distracted.

Why did she fascinate him so much? She was young and pretty, but he knew many beautiful women. He wasn't interested in getting involved with any of them, and they were far more suitable. For one thing, none of them was his employee.

But the last thing he wanted or needed right now was a relationship with anyone. There was just too much to be done. And as for sex, that was easy enough to get without risking commitment, or disappointing anybody's expectations. And even so, those times were very few and far between.

But somehow he found Sabrina impossible to put out of his mind. Perhaps it was her attitude. She was carefree and so different.

He found her delightful and intriguing, and it was beginning to worry him. Ever since meeting her his behavior had been alarming. Maybe Sybil's death had affected him far more than he had acknowledged to himself.

It was hard to mourn a woman who had never loved him, and actively discouraged him from loving her. And he couldn't be a hypocrite and pretend guilt or remorse for that. But he wasn't so stupid as to think that he could come out unscathed. He had a mountain of emotional baggage to deal with.

God knows, his mother had left him a hell of a legacy: Worth's, a tottering dinosaur on the verge of collapse. And, what he found hardest to forgive, a son who treated him like an unwelcome stranger.

Maybe this attraction was some kind of bizarre repercussion. Perhaps his guilt over not feeling real grief had left him vulnerable and ripe to be charmed by a unique personality like Sabrina.

But it was more than just charm. When was the last time he'd felt this lonely? He had always been alone—he was used to it—but she made him feel more keenly conscious of it than ever.

The ping of the elevator brought him back to earth abruptly. He stepped in and punched the button for the top floor. He had to get a grip on reality. It was completely taboo to feel this way about a female employee.

THREE DAYS LATER, at precisely 8:58 p.m., the elevator swept Sabrina silently up to the top floor, while she lectured herself on keeping calm. After all, if he didn't like the designs she carried in her briefcase, that was okay—she had a million more ideas. But that didn't stop her from meticulously checking her reflection in the mirrored walls and plucking tiny bits of fluff off her hot pink silk suit.

It wasn't just his opinion of her work that concerned her. As much as she hated to acknowledge it, she tingled with heady excitement at the thought of seeing Michael again, in spite of all those mental lectures that she was being foolish and asking for trouble.

Stepping off the elevator, her feet sank into the plush carpet as she passed the empty reception desk. It was odd seeing it all deserted, but when she'd called Michael about the display proposals, he'd told her to come up at nine. She usually finished at five but, according to Anya, Michael practically lived in his office.

Sabrina clasped the briefcase handle a little more tightly. Staying late was no inconvenience if it meant the opportunity to pitch her ideas directly to the CEO.

When she walked into the outer office, she noticed Michael's door standing slightly ajar. Through it she could hear a high, rapid voice that she recognized immediately. Colin. The words were indistinct, but there was no mistaking his fury.

Feeling awkward, she moved to step back into the reception area just as he burst out of his father's office. He paused and looked at her for a moment, his young face sullen and pale with rage, then brushed past her.

She turned to see Michael standing in his office doorway, anger burning in his face, but as he watched his son push through the outer doors his eyes filled with a bleak expression that gave her an unexpected jolt of pain. They held the unutterable frustration and worry of a loving parent at his wits' end. It was the first sign of vulnerability she'd seen him betray. The first time she'd seen him in less than total control.

Then he turned and saw her, and instantly the hard mask was back in place, so completely, she could almost believe she'd imagined that pain. But she hadn't. A sudden longing surged through her; she wanted to put her arms around him, to hold him close and comfort him.

"Sabrina, I'm sorry to have kept you waiting. Won't you please come in?"

He was using her first name. The sound of it on his lips gave her an unreasonable thrill. He stood aside to let her walk into the office and, as she passed, his warm, masculine scent enveloped her in a momentary embrace.

She paused uncertainly in the middle of the room. It was lit only by the soft glow of the green-shaded banker's lamp on his desk and another lamp on the oak credenza against one wall. Behind the desk the nighttime city skyline lay, a million tiny jewels of light.

"Won't you please take a seat." Cool and formal, his tone held no trace of the turmoil she'd seen in his expression a moment before.

She sank down into the Queen Anne chair in front of his desk, her legs faintly trembling, her heart racing. It seemed she'd better get used to this feeling whenever Michael was near.

"So what do you have for me?"

As he walked past her to take his seat, just the sound of his husky voice in the quiet room sent a painful shiver over her sensitized skin. She opened her briefcase, ruthlessly willing herself to ignore the tremors still shuddering through her. She had to get control of herself. That feeling was strictly off-limits.

Pulling out the small folder of sketches, she slid it across the desk to him, forcing herself to meet his look with an equally dispassionate gaze. As he reached for the portfolio, his eyes stayed on her while he opened the folder and began pulling out her drawings. She thought her face would crack from the strain of maintaining a neutral expression.

Finally he looked down and slowly began leafing through the sketches. A tiny sigh escaped her lips. One more hurdle passed.

This feeling wasn't something she could take lightly anymore. There had been nothing sexual about that surge of compassion she had felt for him, but it was more frightening than all her wayward fantasies put together. Michael affected her in a way that was out of her control.

Even now she couldn't stop watching his face, her gaze tracing over the strong jawline, the high cheekbones, straight dark brows drawn together in concentration as he carefully perused each sketch. That stray lock of hair had flopped onto his brow again, she noticed, and felt a disturbing wave of tenderness.

Suddenly he looked up and caught her watching him. For a moment his eyes narrowed; then his expression cleared and he gave her a small smile. "Good work."

The quiet words of praise gave her an inordinate rush of pride, out of all proportion to the cause. "You mean you like them?"

Looking at her perched anxiously on the chair, he was suddenly acutely aware that they were all alone, aware of the slow, throbbing heat coursing through him because she was close enough that he could smell her delicate floral scent.

He nodded. She roused his curiosity, but there was something else underneath all that, a nameless longing he didn't want to examine too closely.

"You *really* liked them?"

He couldn't prevent a smile at her exuberance as he drank in the play of soft lamplight on her smooth, silken hair. She was so vibrant, so fresh and alive. She lit up the staid world that was Worth's—*his* staid world.

Sabrina watched in fascination as one dark brow raised a fraction. The firm line of his mouth quirked in one corner and the dimple fluttered as he looked into her eyes; then that slow hint of gentle irony crept into his soft voice. "I *really* liked them."

"Oh..." was all she could manage. But her pleasure was tinged with fear. It might be impossible for her to work with this man at all. How could she cope with these feelings and hope to conceal them?

All at once she realized that she was leaning forward in the chair, betraying her expectant anxiety. She slowly leaned back and tried to look assured and casual, but her eyes were still caught in his clear, direct and lightly mocking gaze.

"I'll have Anya set up a meeting with you, Jonathan and myself. We have a lot to discuss. In fact the timing couldn't be better. Perry St. John-Smythe, Director of Promotions in London, will be coming over soon. We'll schedule it for then." As he spoke, he flipped open the leather-bound calendar on his desk and penciled something in.

Things happened with Michael around, and they happened fast. Even in a few short weeks he'd made substantial changes to the store. And now this. His decisiveness took her breath away.

"Perhaps you could leave your sketches with me so I can look them over at my leisure." The sound of his voice was like warm velvet against her flesh, sending a molten surge of heat through her. And when he looked up, it seemed her heart stopped beating for a moment.

"No problem." She tried to sound light and airy, but her low, throaty voice betrayed her.

His eyes were glittering and intense. The silence lengthened around them. They were all alone up here. Just her and Michael. And something hummed in the air between them. Awareness. And it wasn't just her. He felt it, too. She knew it.

As if he were reaching out and actually touching her, she became aware of the slow, throbbing heat coursing through her. Mind, body, emotion, helplessly caught up in something over which she had no control.

His eyes searched her face and all at once she felt painfully exposed. She must be an open book—all the emotions he inspired laid bare for him to see.

Unable to hold his gaze a second longer, she lunged for her briefcase and moved it onto her lap, clasping the handles tightly. But still he watched her, and her mouth went dry.

She swallowed, trying to keep her voice even. "Was there anything else, Mr. Worth?"

After a small silence he murmured, "No, you may go." But something in his eyes said *Stay*.

No. Either she was mistaken, and projecting her fantasy wishes on him, or he had seen through her flimsy facade and was responding like any red-blooded man to a woman throwing herself at him.

She rose so abruptly, the chair tipped backward on the carpet. "In that case I'll say good-night." She could hear the shameful tremor in her voice.

Michael slowly got to his feet, his eyes still on her stricken face. Now that small derisive smile returned as she hurriedly righted the chair. She couldn't look at him any longer. She might as well have come straight out and said, *I want you.*

As she turned to go, his voice stopped her. "What are you doing working so late on a Friday night?"

She turned back to see him still standing behind the desk, his face in shadow, his eyes faintly glittering in the gloom.

Sabrina shrugged, feeling much too vulnerable to her own wayward emotions. "You asked me to be here."

She heard a soft chuckle. "My God, you only work till five." His lips curved in a smile. "Why didn't you say so?" he murmured, low and intimate.

Oh, God, this wasn't her imagination. "It didn't really matter. I found plenty to do."

"Do you find your work that fulfilling, my loyal Miss Cates?" The gentle mockery in his voice did nothing to quell the little rush of pleasure at being called *his* Miss Cates.

"Yes. I enjoy my work," she said, a trifle too defensively, conscious of him watching her, eyes dark and shadowy in the dim light. The simple and lowering truth was, she'd do just about anything he asked her to.

"But it's after nine o'clock on a Friday night. Don't you date?"

She blinked, then stared at him in astonishment. "I beg your pardon?" That was the last question she'd expected him to ask.

"You're too young to be burying yourself in your work."

"I don't bury myself in my work, and of course I date! Just because I don't have one tonight doesn't mean I don't date." She was so rattled, she was babbling and overly defensive, but she didn't want him thinking she was some kind of lonely, pathetic spinster!

"But what about all the other nights you work late?"

"How do you know about those?"

"There's not much around here I don't know . . . now." He gave her a probing look that made her feel scrutinized right down to her soul. The heat of awareness, growing stronger every second, singed a path right through her.

"What about you? Why don't *you* have a date tonight?" She had a choice. She could either cower in defense, or go on the attack.

"I don't have time to date."

"What about your friend?"

"My friend?" He gave her a puzzled look and she wished she could just drop the whole thing, but she'd come too far now and he was waiting to be enlightened.

"The woman—I mean, your friend in the limo the other evening." Somebody really *should* cut out her tongue! But that pair of legs had haunted her dreams. Who was that woman Michael was close to?

His expression cleared, and once again there was that hint of derision in his smile. "Oh, you mean Katherine."

Yes, Katherine. She realized with a sense of shock that she was intensely jealous of Katherine. And all she was so far was a pair of legs and a name.

"We're old friends. She kindly stepped into the breach when I needed an escort. I was meeting a potential new supplier for dinner and he was bringing his wife along."

"Oh, I see." She kept on doing it! Putting her foot in it, or laying her most embarrassing thoughts bare for him to trample on.

Even through the gloom she could feel his keen eyes probing hers. "Katherine is particularly good in those sorts of situations. She's done a lot of business entertaining for her father."

"Oh . . ."

"As for dating, my work consumes me and I like it that way."

The low, dispassionate statement had the definite ring of a door clanging shut, but she couldn't hold back the barbed mimicry. "Aren't you too young to be burying yourself in your work?"

"I've never been too young," he said lightly, but his mouth twisted in self-mockery on the words, and suddenly she saw through him, through all the trappings of power, to the deep core of loneliness. *That* was the essence of him. That was what held him apart.

Who was this man? She searched his face, desperately wanting to know, but his expression was veiled in the dim light.

"I'm sorry." The words came out without her being aware she'd spoken.

"About what?" His voice sharpened, one eyebrow rose warily.

"All the responsibilities you have to bear. They probably started at a very young age."

The threat vanished. He began to chuckle. "Sort of poor little rich boy, huh?"

He shook his head and grinned with malicious hardness, mocking her for being a fool, for thinking that someone with his armor would need her pity. It hurt to have her compassion thrown back in her face.

"I'm sorry." Her throat tightened; she felt tears burn behind her eyes and quickly turned before he saw them and misconstrued the reason.

Before she had taken two blind steps, he moved swiftly and silently around the desk to stop her with a hand on her arm, gruff and slightly apologetic. "What are you sorry for this time?"

Her pounding heart was making her breathless. Feeling his fingers curled around her, the heat of his body so close to hers, she could barely speak. "For being so presumptuous."

She heard him sigh; then he turned her around with both hands and looked down into her face. She couldn't hide the tears in her eyes, making his face shimmer in the dim light.

He gave a sigh of impatience and his hands—warm, gentle hands—framed her face. "I'm sorry. I didn't mean to make you cry."

Blinking the tears away, she saw his remorse, but now the hunger in his eyes was no longer veiled; it burned down into her like a scorching flame. But with a cold, bleak edge that told her he didn't want to feel the attraction any more than she did.

"I think I'd better go home now," she murmured, but found herself leaning toward him instead of pulling away. Now she knew for certain he wanted her to stay, but that would be lunacy.

His voice was barely a whisper. "Yes, I think it's best that you leave."

Without conscious thought she stepped toward him and heard his sharp indrawn breath. One hand slid around to cup the back of her head and bring her gently but inexorably closer.

The moment she felt his mouth on hers, her body seemed to melt and go up in flames at the same time. Like a moment she'd been waiting for forever. And yet she seemed to know his kiss already, knew the shape of his lips with the intimacy of a lover.

His male scent invaded her senses and she sighed, feeling his firm, hard mouth softening, clinging to hers. Dizzying sensations went shivering through her. She eagerly opened her mouth to his plunging ravishment, glad of his supporting arms wrapped tightly around her. As their tongues entwined, she shuddered with an intensity of feeling that went beyond pleasure, to become almost excruciating. She clung tighter as a little moan escaped her throat.

Michael broke away abruptly, grasping her shoulders to put her away from him, and she saw the stunned realization in his eyes.

What were they doing? Shocked at her own instinctive, shameless response, Sabrina moved quickly backward.

Michael turned away and ran a hand through his hair. On shaking legs, she stepped over to pick up her briefcase and turned back to see him watching her, determination in his eyes.

His chest rose and fell rapidly, but obviously he had already begun mastering the physical reaction. His voice was firm, bearing only a slight betraying trace of raggedness. "It would be useless to deny that I'm attracted to you, but it won't go any further, I can promise you that. I can't afford a sexual harassment suit."

She felt as if he'd plunged a knife in her breast. Sabrina strove to control her shaky breathing and cleared her throat. "Sexual harassment! We both know it was mutual."

"Yes, but what's to prevent you from turning around later and saying I forced you to submit to me, by threatening you with the loss of your job?"

"I'll tell you what's to prevent me." Her voice was shaking with anger as he gave the knife another twist. "My honesty and scruples!"

"Calm down. I'm not suggesting that you would." He gave her a weary, cynical smile. "But when it comes to money, it's easy for greed to supplant scruples. I'm a very wealthy man and an obvious target for something like that. Although I can afford the best legal talent in the country. The charges would never stick."

He felt like a bastard. And that was exactly what he wanted her to think of him. It was the only way to protect her from himself.

Deep down inside he'd wanted that kiss to happen—he knew that now. He was disgusted with his own hypocrisy and a little afraid that she could make him lose his self-control so easily. From now on, Sabrina Cates was off-limits, *completely* off-limits. Even in his thoughts.

"Then what are you afraid of?" The scary thing was, she could see that in his position such a suspicion was all too reasonable. And she'd be perfectly willing to understand if she weren't so hurt by the implication that she would stoop so low. But he didn't *know* her. She had to remember that.

"I can't afford the time and the distraction of a messy court battle. So therefore I think it best we forget about this unfortunate incident."

"You won't get an argument from me. I wish it had never happened!" Bitterness left a sick feeling in the pit of her stomach. How could he think she'd resort to something so cold, calculating and underhanded as to deliberately entrap him?

"So do I. And please don't take it personally. If anyone's to blame, it's me. I broke one of my own cardinal rules."

"It's very big of you to take all the responsibility," she said sarcastically.

She felt crushed. If she could sense instinctively that he was decent and honorable, shouldn't he be perceptive enough to know the same of her? Of course, over the past weeks, he'd consumed her every waking thought. It was unreasonable to imagine he would have invested the same amount of time trying to figure *her* out.

He shoved his hands into his trouser pockets and turned abruptly toward the window that looked down on the traffic of Queen Street and the Old City Hall beyond, its contours picked out in lights like a fairy-tale castle.

"So are we agreed that our best course of action would be to ignore this . . . this unfortunate incident?"

"Yes." Thank God for the pride that came to her rescue, firming her voice.

He nodded toward the view. "Good night, Sabrina." His quiet words had a ring of finality.

It was easy for him. All he had to fight was an unwanted, unwelcome physical attraction. For her it had already transcended the physical. But she could do it. She had to. She should just thank God he was the kind of hard, controlled man who could keep matters like this in ruthless perspective.

"Good night, Mr. Worth."

Her head held high, she turned to leave. But at the door something made her stop and look back. Michael still stood at the window, looking out on the lights below, his hands still shoved into his pockets. A powerful man with the world at his feet. But, despite how deeply he had hurt her, all she could feel at this moment was the sharp, painful conviction of his loneliness.

He turned and saw her dark eyes clouded with genuine concern and pain, and it almost broke his heart. But for that reason he deliberately turned back to the window. He held his breath until he heard the soft click of the door as she left.

Why? Why did he let it go that far? He felt like shit. Not just because of what he'd done but because, even now, he wanted to go after her and call her back, plead with her not to leave him alone. He didn't want to be alone anymore.

He ran a hand through his hair and let out his breath. What was happening to him? Maybe he was just punchy from the constant commuting to London, and the stress of running two stores an ocean apart.

And then he remembered that white-hot surge of desire, stunning in its intensity. For those few moments he was just feeling, not thinking at all. It was disturbingly reminiscent of the early days with Lorraine, and the consequences of that mistake had changed the path of his entire life.

He had had an excuse then: he was just a kid. But he could never allow himself to have his judgment clouded like that again. And yet, even knowing all that, the desire was still there, with an insistency that scared him. But it had to be ruthlessly ignored.

It might be too late already, a small voice warned him. Already the seeds of discontent were taking root. For the first time in his life he wanted more.

4

SABRINA POURED hot salsa into a bowl, put it on the tray beside the bag of nacho chips and headed for the living room. Maybe it wasn't a balanced meal, but it was all she had the energy to make right now, after a long Saturday working overtime.

A knock sounded at the door and she got up with a sigh. Unexpected company was the last thing she needed at the moment. She just wanted to laze about for the evening.

Through the lace curtain covering the small window in the door she saw Colin's face and suddenly felt even more tired. She leaned her forehead against the cool white-painted wood. Didn't the boy know when to stop?

Taking a deep breath, she opened the door. "Colin, what are you doing here?" The words weren't very welcoming, but she didn't care. The last few weeks of being gentle and tactful had got her nowhere.

But he didn't seem to notice her sharpness. "He can't do this to me." His voice sounded uneven and shaky as she followed him into the room. He stopped and turned to face her.

"Who can't do what to you?"

"My father, that's who." He took a deep breath, but he was shuddering and his lips quivered as if he were fighting back tears. "He's cut off my allowance. He says from now on if I want money, I've got to earn it."

Her mouth fell open in disbelief. Here she'd been thinking someone had died, but in fact he was just throwing a king-size temper tantrum!

"I have to work at the store all summer, and part-time when school starts. I start Monday morning in the stockroom. And do you know what I'll be doing?" His face contorted with bitterness as his voice rose to an outraged squeak. "I'll be in charge of garbage!"

Her compassion evaporated and she felt like laughing. "What's wrong with that?"

Bravo for Michael. Personally, she thought putting Colin to work was exactly what he needed. Being indulged and idle wasn't good for anybody's character.

He stared at her as if she'd just sprouted another head. "What's right about it? He told me I had to learn the business from the ground up. It's so damn degrading." He ground out the last words between his teeth.

"Nothing about working is degrading. What's really degrading is taking money for nothing."

The blank look on his face told her that he hadn't a clue what she meant. All his life he'd been handed anything he wanted. Who could blame him if he thought it was his God-given right to just take?

"But he's trying to humiliate me," Colin insisted. "If he had to put me to work, why not in Promotions? I helped you last summer."

"Yes, I remember," she said wryly. "Every time I needed you, you were off gallivanting somewhere. The truth is, Colin, you weren't much of a help." It looked like there was no alternative to ruthless honesty.

"But the stockroom!" The belligerence had died away and now he simply looked shattered. "He hates me."

"He doesn't hate you." She let out a patient sigh. "He just wants you to learn the business from the ground up, like he did. What's wrong with that?"

"My grandmother was teaching me the business, and she didn't expect me to work in the stockroom. He has no right to do this to me," he ground out, getting himself all worked up again.

"I'm afraid he has every right," Sabrina said quietly, and lifted her hand to smooth back the silky blond hair from his forehead, then slipped her arm around his shoulder to give him a reassuring squeeze. "He's your father."

"Some father." With a bitter laugh he pulled away from her abruptly. He began pacing toward the window, then spun around to face her with an accusing glare. "The guy dumped me with my grandmother, then went off to forget about me for the next seventeen years."

She stared back at him in shock. Was Michael really capable of callously abandoning his child? No, she couldn't believe, even from the little she'd seen, that he was a man to walk away from his responsibilities.

"I know it must be very difficult to suddenly have this stranger descend on you, but you haven't given yourself much time to adjust to having your father around...."

"He's no stranger. He's back and forth all the time. As a matter of fact, he's always popping up where I don't want him to, pretending he cares about me."

"Make up your mind, Colin. Did he abandon you or not?" She was rapidly becoming exasperated with this boy. She gave him a hard look. "I think you're exaggerating, don't you?"

Tight-lipped with resentment, he didn't reply. Sabrina went over to where he stood by the window. She had to make him see reality. Looking up into his flushed face, she saw the low slanting beams of sunlight gleaming on his taut skin, revealing the fine downy fuzz on his cheeks. He was so young. Something inside her softened. She wouldn't want to be seventeen again for anything in the world.

She reached for his hands, but he pulled them away, shoving them into his shorts pockets as he turned to look out the window.

"You know, Colin," she said more gently, "you should stop and think about all the advantages you've had...."

"What advantages?" He wheeled around, bitterness etched on his face.

"Money, education..."

He snorted in derision.

"Hey, don't knock them," she said sharply. "I know it's going to be an adjustment earning your living. But it's no more than most people have to do, every day of their lives."

"He's trying to ruin my life." Now he sounded more forlorn than defiant as he twisted away from her and flopped down on the couch to bury his face in his hands.

Despite her frustration, she had to smile a little to herself at his sense of drama. Maybe it wasn't such a bad thing that he'd brought his problem to her. He obviously needed someone to talk to.

She went to sit down beside him. "I think he's just trying to help you grow up."

From outside, she heard the dull squeak of the screen door being yanked open, then three hard raps on the brass knocker. Getting to her feet, she stepped over to the door. Her heart came up into her throat when she met the blazing anger in Michael's eyes on the other side of the sheer lace curtain.

She slowly opened the door.

"I apologize for the intrusion, but I've come to get my son." He seemed to look right through her, implacable as granite, the fury tightly leashed in his harsh, cold voice.

"Of course. Won't you come in?" The sheer force of his anger made her tremble inside. What would happen if that iron control snapped?

Glacial eyes slid away from her as he stepped past her into the room.

"What are you doing here?" Colin had jumped to his feet, his fist clenching, and the familiar sullen hostility in his face.

A cold hand clutched the pit of her stomach at the sound of Michael's grim, low voice.

"What do you think I'm doing here?"

Even now there was no letting go of the terrible inner control. It was almost inhuman. It frightened her. She couldn't believe this was the same man who'd kissed her, who had lost himself, even for a few moments.

But then again, she *could* believe it. His passions would go to extremes, whatever they were, but he would always keep them ruthlessly under control.

"How did you know where to find me?" Two bright spots of color burned on Colin's pale face and his eyes were rimmed with red.

"I followed you. And it wasn't easy."

The boy looked such a pathetic mixture of youth, hurt and defiance. Why couldn't Michael just go over and put his arm around his son? Why couldn't they work things out without all this seething antagonism? Why couldn't he relax that iron control? Why couldn't life be that simple?

"Couldn't have been that hard. You're here, aren't you?" Colin sneered.

"I have a few comments to make on your driving, but we'll save that for later. Right now you're going to get into your car and go home and we will finish the discussion we started earlier."

"No. I don't want to." Colin stared past him.

It seemed impossible for Michael's face to harden further, but she saw the muscles working as his chiseled jaw tightened, mouth thinning to an implacable line. His quiet voice sent an icy shiver up her spine. "I don't remember asking you."

"You can't force me to do anything." The belligerence was fading from Colin's glare. "I'm not a kid anymore. I'll do what I please."

"You'll do what I tell you. Now let's go." Michael's quiet, almost conversational tone didn't hide the steel in his voice. "We have plenty to discuss, but we're not going to do it here, and we've taken up enough of Miss Cates's time."

"No!" The defiance in Colin's face was now mingled with uncertainty. "Anything you have to say, you can say in front of Sabrina." His voice quivered dangerously.

Quietly she cleared her throat. "No, Colin. Do what your father says."

Colin's sullen gaze slid away. With his mouth clamped tight and his shoulders rigid, he walked out the door, brushing past her without another glance.

Now Michael turned his relentless gaze on her and she flinched. The force of his anger was as tangible as a slap in the face. "You think I'm a bastard, don't you?"

A spasm of pain tore through her. "Of course not," she gasped.

His eyes flashed scorn and skepticism. "It's fairly obvious your sympathies are with Colin."

"As a matter of fact, I think you did the right thing." It was hard to breathe, she could feel her heart pounding against her ribs.

"Thank you."

The cold derision in his voice brought a flush to her cheeks and a sharp pain to her chest, but like it or not, she was involved.

"However... perhaps..." She faltered, not wanting to meet the expression in his eyes. "There are better and worse ways of broaching certain things."

"In other words, I acted like a jerk."

"I didn't say that," she put in quickly, meeting his cold challenge and feeling as if she were walking on quicksand. Getting caught between father and son was the last thing she wanted, but she was being dragged in, willy-nilly. "And I'm not trying to tell you how to deal with your son. I was just trying to help, but... it's none of my business," she finished lamely, wishing with all her heart that she hadn't been put in this miserable position.

He fixed her with a long unreadable look. When he finally spoke, his tone was formal, dismissive. "I'm sorry you had to be bothered with all this."

He went to follow his son, but some mad urge impelled her to reach out and stop him with a hand on his arm. A warm tingling spread from her fingertips and settled in her abdomen.

"I know how difficult this must be for you, but I think you're on the right track."

He looked down at her hand and then gently, but firmly, removed it. "I don't need your pity."

His eyes glinted dark blue steel as they held hers; then he walked out, leaving her aching from that absolute rejection, and more unnerved than she could ever remember being.

Even after she closed the door, she couldn't erase the last glimpse of Michael's face. Under all that anger and hardness lay a depth of pain and loneliness that would go on haunting her, even in her dreams.

FOR THE NEXT TWO WEEKS she didn't see much of Michael, except from a distance. He was everywhere, overseeing the renovations.

They'd stripped the columns of the tacky mirrors that some bright spark in the sixties had probably thought were really groovy, cleaned the grime of decades from the molded plaster and regilded the Corinthian capitals, as they had been back in the twenties. At the same time all the battered parquet floors were being ripped up and replaced by beautiful verdigris Italian marble.

Michael kept a close eye on the work in progress, but when she did see him striding down the aisles, that dark head never turned in her direction. Although she carried the memory of that night at her house like a weight in her heart, the chances were that he'd already forgotten her role in that exchange with his son. After all, she meant nothing to him, had no part in his life.

But now, as she stood beside him in Worth's suburban warehouse, which housed the parade floats, once again she was hit with that sledgehammer awareness.

The familiar sounds of sawing and banging, and the calls of the workmen filled her ears. The smell of glue and freshly cut wood met her nostrils. Sunlight came pouring in, illuminating brilliantly colored floats.

Yet she was much more aware of Michael keeping pace beside her as they walked down the aisle between the floats. The heat of his body, that tangible energy emanating from him. There was no getting away from the effect he had on her.

He paused and looked curiously at a bright yellow crescent made of cut foam.

"The Cow Jumps Over the Moon," she rushed to explain. If she kept her eyes on her floats, on anything but him, maybe she could cut through the sensual haze that seemed to envelop her in his presence.

Remember, kiddo, she told herself, he's your boss, and showing him the parade floats under construction was part of her job. She wasn't here to indulge in reckless fantasies.

"And there's the cow." Looking up from the yellow-painted moon, she pointed above their heads to a life-size Guernsey that hung suspended from the ceiling. "This year we're doing nursery rhymes and fairy tales. And over there—" she pointed to the wooden frame of a small house, where a workman was draping the roof with cardboard painted to resemble red tiles "—The Farmer in the Dell."

From the corner of her eye she watched Michael walk around the half-finished structure. In his pale gray suit, snowy white shirt and perfect grooming he looked conspicuously out of place in this blue-collar environment. Out of place and very sexy. Surely there was some law against looking so wonderful.

"It looks good, doesn't it?" He ran a keen, critical glance over the hillbilly shack, and a surprised smile broke out on his face, a carefree curve of his mouth that made the dimple crease his cheek.

She nodded as a shudder went through her in response to that intoxicating smile. God, this was going to be so hard.

"Takes you back," she murmured in a desperate effort to make conversation and take her mind off her own reaction.

He looked perplexed. "To what?"

"Childhood, of course," she said with a stilted laugh.

"Maybe yours. Not my childhood." He gave a slight shake of his head and turned away toward the float.

The quiet matter-of-fact words left her wondering. What kind of a mother had Sybil been? Had he been a child at all? Compassion welled up in her. From all that she'd seen and heard, Sybil Worth had been a coldhearted autocrat. Her adored Colin had been the only one who seemed to have the power to thaw her.

"What have we got here?" Michael's husky voice brought her back to earth and she found him looking up at a towering castle, complete with turrets and colorful pennants.

"Ah! *This* is my pièce de résistance."

She stepped over to a man wielding a paintbrush, putting in highlights and shadows in various shades of gray. "Hi, Harry. How's it going?"

"Just fine." He added a few more artful brush strokes and suddenly a block of granite materialized on the canvas. "Looks pretty good now, doesn't it?"

"It sure does." She turned to Michael with a conspiratorial smile. "This is the original Cinderella float from the forties." It gave her a rush of pleasure and excitement to see how well it was taking shape. She walked around it, running a critical eye over the old float. "Isn't it great? I dug it out of the back of the warehouse last spring. A lot of the canvas had rotted and the wooden frame needed a bit of repair, but that was all. It's going to be fabulous. Just wait till you see it with the prince and Cinderella! Brocade and velvet and spangles . . ."

"It looks great. Everything looks great."

Something in his voice brought her gaze back to him. He was watching her with a warm admiration that made her feel intensely self-conscious.

She smiled shyly. "Thank you. It's a lot of fun, and so rewarding. I love to watch the faces, kids and adults alike, when the parade goes by." She probably sounded like a sentimental idiot, but she couldn't help herself.

He shot her a swift curious look, then focused on the large, bright red brick wall on his right that, at closer inspection, proved to be made of painted foam.

"Humpty Dumpty." She supplied the explanation with her gaze fixed on the wall, intensely conscious of Michael close beside her.

She heard him sigh and turned to see him looking down at her, his brow furrowed in a troubled frown, a dark, unreadable expression filling his eyes.

"Sabrina, about that unpleasant scene at your house..."

She turned away, wishing he hadn't brought it up. She couldn't think about her meddling without feeling embarrassed. It wasn't her place to say anything about the problems between him and Colin, much less give him advice about child rearing.

"I see you're still angry with me about it."

She spun around in surprise. "Angry with you? Of course not!" His searching expression was hard to meet, and her gaze dropped until she was examining the toes of her cream pumps. "I'm the one who should be apologizing. For sticking my nose in."

"It's a very nice nose." At his quiet, intimate tone she looked up to see a rueful smile. "It's not hard to see why Colin would go to you instead of me."

There was no mistaking the warm intimacy in his voice a moment before, and her heart was still doing flip-flops in her chest. "He thought he'd get a sympathetic ear, but I'm afraid all he got from me was an earful."

"Poor Colin." But his smile was full of warm admiration.

"Poor Michael." The words tumbled out before she could stop them.

"Why do you say that?" The smile faded and he was watching her closely.

Once again she had talked herself into a corner. "I...I know Colin's behavior must be hard to cope with."

"Don't feel too sorry for me." His mouth twisted in self-contempt. "I made my bed, and now I have to lie in it."

Once again, he didn't want her pity. But he had aroused her curiosity even more. Then he turned to her and smiled, and suddenly she was forcibly reminded of all those unsettling feelings always simmering beneath the surface, and why that curiosity was a dangerous thing to indulge.

A slow-burning fire was spreading through her from deep inside, a nameless emotion she couldn't identify. And with it a slight chill descended on her.

Somehow she had crossed the line into completely new territory. This was no longer just a physical attraction she could tease herself with. Her feelings were becoming much too intense for comfort.

FOR THE NEXT FEW WEEKS, however, she had a welcome respite while Michael went back to the London store. The days crawled by and then he returned, and all those feelings she had thought doused by the passage of time were back full force.

As he'd promised, he'd brought Perry St. John-Smythe, the Director of Promotions from London, back with him to see the renovations in progress and to meet with her and Jonathan.

The meeting had been very successful, in spite of her distraction. She'd come to the gloomy realization that as long as Michael was around, it was something she'd have to learn to cope with. But even as he sat behind his desk listening silently to the proceedings, he'd been a more compelling presence than either of the two men flanking her. And they were both pretty high-powered individuals—not exactly chopped liver. But with Michael around...

She hurried toward the door to catch up with Jonathan when Perry's voice stopped her.

"So, Sabrina, would it be too pushy of me to ask you to show me around this lovely city of yours?"

She turned to see his smiling hazel eyes on her, as they had been incessantly since she met him for the first time that morning. Her gaze instinctively flew to Michael sitting behind his desk, watching impassively, giving no clue what he thought of Perry's obvious interest.

With his upper-crust name, and his responsible position, she'd expected some sort of toffee-nosed, bowler-topped stereotype of an Englishman. But the blond, good-looking Perry had proved to be in his early thirties and dressed with fashionable dash, without in any way sacrificing his masculinity.

Michael still gave no response. What did she expect? A display of possessiveness?

"Sure, I'd love to," she said quickly, wrenching her gaze away to focus on Perry.

She cared far too much about what Michael might think and feel. She sternly reminded herself that it didn't matter. She had to stop thinking about Michael, period. Perhaps showing Perry around would offer a distraction.

"That's super." He grinned and turned to Michael. "Knowing what a decent chap you are, I know you'll give Sabrina the rest of the day off so we can start now."

"Oh...I...um...I don't think so," she interjected, feeling very embarrassed.

"Go ahead." Michael cut her off acerbically. He turned to Perry. "I think we could spare Sabrina for a few hours."

She bridled a little at the high-handed way they were arranging her time. Obviously she was expected to go along with it.

"Thanks a bundle." She didn't try very hard to suppress the hint of sarcasm in her voice. Perry didn't seem to notice, but she saw Michael's raised eyebrow.

Perhaps this was just what she needed. For the past few weeks she'd been trapped in this miserable self-imposed prison of her own emotions, her mind always revolving around Michael. She needed to forget about him, at least for a few hours, and refused to acknowledge the thought that, with the two men being close friends, she might learn more about him from Perry.

"Great." Perry came over and cupped her elbow. "But let's not hang around here, in case he changes his mind."

A quick glance at Michael found him watching her once more, with that unrevealing stare.

"Well, then, let's go." She tried to contain the sudden rise of irritation. What did she expect him to say? You can't go out with her because she's mine?

As she turned to go, she heard Perry murmur behind her back. "Thanks, old boy, I owe you one. Don't wait up for me."

Her mouth curled with a grim smile. Whatever Perry might have in mind, the only good time she intended to show him was a tour of the city sights.

THE NEXT MORNING, Sabrina bolted off the elevator at the executive suite, ten minutes late for her 9:00 a.m. meeting. How could she have forgotten to set her alarm?

But it had been nearly one when she fell into bed, exhausted from showing Perry the town. Given his enthusiastic interest, she'd been rather glad about her previously arranged dinner date with Anya. She'd sensed the disappointment under Perry's polite charm, but over dinner he and Anya had quickly taken to each other. By the time she called it a night, they were heading off together to enjoy the nightlife on Queen Street.

She dashed into the boardroom to find Michael, Jonathan and Perry already seated at the long, gleaming table.

"I'm sorry I'm late," she said breathlessly, and closed the heavy door behind her.

"I'm surprised you managed to make it at all after your...satisfying evening." There was a slight restraint in Michael's manner, an edge to his voice that gave her a moment's pause, but she felt too tired to put much trust in her perceptions.

She sank into the high-backed old chair next to Jonathan. Perry sat across the table and she noticed that he looked even more tired than she felt. There were dark shadows under his eyes and she was positive he was wearing the same suit and tie as the day before.

Despite her best intentions, during their time together, she'd found herself asking him about Michael. It had turned out that they had met while attending Oxford, and were close enough friends that he was staying at Michael's house. All he basically told her was that Michael lived and breathed Worth's, but she already knew that.

"Jonathan, perhaps you can start by bringing us up to date . . ."

Without further ado, Michael began the meeting. First thing in the morning and he looked as sharp and dynamic as always in his navy suit and crisp white shirt, exuding power and vitality in tangible waves. The formal attire that made other men look stuffy made him look sexy.

It also made her even more conscious of how hurriedly she had thrown on her white damask suit and rushed to work.

Throughout the meeting, she kept noticing his eyes on her, filled with a brooding intensity that made her acutely uncomfortable. It was so difficult to concentrate on what the others were saying that she knew she'd have to ask Jonathan for a recap later.

Finally it was over and they rose to leave. But as she reached the door, Michael's cool voice stopped her. "Sabrina, would you stay for a moment, please? I'd like a word with you."

Perry and Jonathan filed past her and the door closed behind them. Slowly she turned toward Michael, feeling once more that now-familiar electric tingle in her limbs, the awareness of being alone with him that made it so difficult to concentrate on anything else.

He stood staring out the window, his back to her. She returned to the chair she had just vacated. When he turned, his face was a grim mask. A quiver of alarm shot through her. What could have happened to change Michael into this hard-faced stranger?

"Did you have a good time last night?"

She stared at him for a moment, trying to correlate the look on his face with the innocuous question. "It was fun," she answered slowly.

"Fun," he repeated, with a mocking laugh. "Just fun? Perry must be losing his touch."

Shock reverberated through her. There was no denying now the latent fury in every harsh syllable. She'd sensed it from the moment she'd walked into the room, but had attributed her unease to tiredness, anxiety and to the overzealous need to be tuned in to him.

"I beg your pardon?"

He stepped toward her with an insolent expression as he stood by his chair at the head of the table. "Perry prides himself on his sexual prowess. I think he'd be most insulted that you found him merely fun."

His words made her go cold. "What exactly do you mean?"

"I mean, I would expect you to be more euphoric. Is that why you were late? You hadn't come back down to earth yet?"

"I don't like what you're implying."

"Perhaps you thought I wouldn't find out. Did you forget Perry was staying with me? He didn't even make it home to change this morning."

"So you assumed he'd been with me!"

"A natural enough assumption, seeing you'd spent the day together."

It was the final painful irony. She'd spent the whole evening unable to stop thinking that she would rather be with him! Perry might be handsome and charming, but now that Michael had entered her heart, no other man would do.

"I see." A surge of anger momentarily overwhelmed her pain. "But I still don't understand why we're discussing this. What does it have to do with you?"

His jaw tightened; one hand gripped the top of his chair until the knuckles went white. "I thought I'd made it quite clear." The icy voice was low and controlled, too controlled. "Even though he's only here for a short time, he's still an employee of Worth's and so are you. Business and personal relationships don't mix."

"Does that mean personal relationships aren't allowed?"

"What do you think?"

She ignored the question with a cold, steely look. "Is this company policy? Does it say in the book of rules somewhere that employees can't have personal relationships with each other?"

"Common sense should tell you that."

"So it's not actually policy? So actually I can do anything I damn well want."

Unrestrained anger flared in his eyes. "How did Perry manage to make it in on time? Or perhaps you got stuck with the breakfast dishes. A friendly word of advice—English men aren't terribly liberated."

She clenched her hands until the nails dug into her palms. "Before you go any further, you'd better get your facts straight."

She was shaking with emotion as she turned to go, then abruptly turned back. Her pride wouldn't let her refute the accusation, but she couldn't walk away without telling him how wrong he was. Despite everything, it still mattered what he thought of her.

She strode around the table and jabbed at the polished surface. "And just for your information, I don't make a habit of going to bed with men I've only known for a day."

"Then where the hell was he all night?"

He leaned toward her, only inches away, the heat from his body wreaking havoc on her. She felt utterly defeated by her response to him, despite everything. She felt like bursting into tears, but she'd rather be drawn and quartered than show that kind of weakness.

"You'll have to ask Perry," she said quietly. It wasn't until this moment that she realized he must have stayed with Anya.

The sudden silence seemed to reverberate with her words as he stared down at her.

"You know I won't do that."

"Why?" she asked acidly. "Would that be a breach of some gentleman's code of honor?"

"Something like that" came the terse reply.

"Oh, I see. You won't insult Perry by giving him the third degree, but I guess I just don't matter." The tears burned hot behind her eyes, and she struggled to fight them back. She snapped her fingers in his face. "Well, *that's* how much I care about your stupid code!" Her vision blurred as she snapped her fingers again. "And *that's* how much I care about you!"

She began to spin away from him. The next thing she knew his fingers had curled around her upper arm in a painful grip and he was pulling her toward him. She struggled to get away, blinded by tears, but his lips came down hard on hers. It took less than a moment for her anger to change to a burning, overwhelming desire that made the hands that had tried to push him away curl into his chest.

She thought he whispered her name against her mouth. It sounded like a plea, but she wasn't sure—the sound of her own heartbeat was drowning out everything else.

At the very first touch, her body caught fire. With a little moan she opened her mouth to his, moving closer, molding herself against the length of him. He gave a deep, shuddering sigh as his arms went around her, lifting her almost off her feet

He lifted her higher, kissing the line of her jaw, her throat, rapidly descending until she felt his mouth hot and feverish on the swell of her breast through the silk blouse.

"If only you knew," he groaned, "how often I've dreamed... of you, like this...." With a frustrated moan he lowered her until she stood on tiptoe, and sought her mouth again. "And more," he murmured against her lips, pulling her tightly to him while his mouth ground against hers, hard and hungry, almost punishing.

Nothing mattered now but Michael, his hot, demanding mouth on hers filling her with a heady, intoxicating lethargy.

Arms wrapped tightly around him, she clung to him, feeling the muscles of his back under her hands, sensing the restraint that battled with his hunger. She returned his kiss with a matching need and passion.

His hands ran over her, arousing every sensitized inch of her body. His lean fingers kneaded her breast through the silk, ran down her back to cup her bottom and pull her closer. She could feel him against her stomach, and a moist, demanding pressure surged between her thighs, urging her against him. She ached to feel him closer, harder and more completely. She wanted everything.... She reached down and ran her hand over his arousal.

He went very still, closing his lips against hers. A sickening, painful jolt shot through her and she strained away from him.

Slowly he lowered her to her feet. She stared at the buttons on his crisp white shirt, unable to look at him, painfully conscious of his tension, his stillness. Ever since they met she'd been playing with fire, and she only had herself to blame for what had happened.

"Sabrina." His voice was low and strained, but in control.

"Please, Michael, don't say anything." She moved away, casting a quick glance at his face to see a dull red staining his cheekbones. "And you needn't be afraid I'll start yelling sexual harassment."

"Please. I've regretted that stupid accusation ever since I uttered it."

"That's a relief. So that's the end of that. There's nothing more to say."

"No, damn it!" He closed his eyes and took a deep, shaky breath, then opened them and frowned at her. "What happened between us a moment ago—"

"Should be forgotten," she interrupted, "and the sooner the better."

"It's not that simple." He let out a frustrated sigh and turned away from her, smoothing a hand over the short hairs on his nape. Her lips trembled to caress the spot. "I thought I could keep this attraction under control."

His low words made her stomach muscles clench in a painful knot. "Don't blame yourself. It takes two hands to clap."

He spun around. "It would spell disaster for both of us if we allowed ourselves to get . . . involved."

"I agree."

"The reason I've steered clear of involvements of any kind is because I don't know of any woman who would willingly take a back seat to my job. Unless you're interested in a one-night stand, which I don't think you are, I suggest we don't take this any further."

"You're right." Her voice sounded surprisingly calm, betraying little of her pain and turmoil churning. And she could add a few reasons of her own why anything between them could never work.

They had nothing in common, except this mutual physical attraction. They came from two different worlds. She already knew that she wouldn't be satisfied with just sex, and more than that, she couldn't have.

He watched her for a long moment, a distant frown in his eyes, his expression unreadable. "I'm glad we see eye to eye on this. Makes life so much less complicated, don't you agree?"

"Yes." She gave him a numb smile. He was attracted to her, but only in the physical sense. "Now if you don't mind, I've got stacks of work waiting for me. I'd better get to it."

"Me, too." He gave her another long searching look, and holding it was the hardest thing she had ever done. "Perhaps it would be better for you to consult with Jonathan from now on, if you have any questions about these new display ideas. It would make things much easier."

"Yes, I agree."

She turned to leave. Yes, it would make things easier, but not seeing him, not having the chance to be close to him for even a few fleeting moments, would be heart wrenching.

She made it back to her office, locked the door behind her and flung herself into the chair. Sinking her head on her hands, she finally let the hot tears flow.

This must be what it felt like when your heart was breaking, she thought. And she couldn't bear it. She had fallen in love with Michael Worth.

5

THAT EVENING, Sabrina walked slowly down her quiet tree-lined street in the warm summer breeze, paying scant attention to the familiar sight due south—the wooden boardwalk, the swathe of sand and then the glittering blue of Lake Ontario.

She had been lost in thought as she came home from work on the streetcar, to her pleasant Beaches neighborhood in the east end. Again and again, she replayed those moments in the boardroom and came to the same conclusion: she was in love.

As she drew closer to her tiny redbrick duplex, she was surprised to see Colin sitting on the porch. He spotted her and came bounding down the steps.

"Hello, Colin. What are you doing here?" She smiled up at him, seeing him somehow differently now. He was Michael's son. And being in love with Michael made Colin even more precious to her.

"I've been waiting for you." He grinned, vibrating with pent-up excitement. "Aren't you going to ask me why I'm here?" Colin shifted his lanky frame from foot to foot, obviously so excited, he could hardly keep still.

"I did, but I'll ask you again. What are you doing here?" She smiled at him with an indulgent surge of affection.

"I've got a surprise for you. Come and see." He grabbed her arm.

"Hey, easy on. That arm happens to be attached to the rest of me." With a good-natured laugh, she pulled out of his grasp.

"I have a surprise for you that just can't wait. Please, Sabrina." He tugged at her hand impatiently.

"Okay." She grinned. "What have you got to show me?"

Colin pulled her a little farther along the sidewalk, then stopped. "Well?" He stood back with a satisfied smile curving his lips, like the cat who'd got the cream.

"Well, what?" She stared at him, mystified.

"Well...do you like it?" He beamed from ear to ear and patted the roof of the green Miata parked in front of his black Porsche that was a present from his indulgent grandmother.

Sabrina glanced at the little sports car, then turned back with a smile. "It's very nice."

He stood grinning at her for a moment as if he were about to explode with excitement. "Well, it's yours!"

He dug into his pocket and pulled out a set of keys, dangling them in front of her.

Sabrina could only gasp. "What?"

"It's yours." His eyes bright and expectant, he waited to enjoy her reaction.

"What do you mean, it's mine?" A sick churning began in her stomach.

"That's my surprise. I bought it for you." He took her unresisting hand and led her around to the front. "See!" He pointed proudly to the license plate that read SABRINA.

"You bought it for me?" She gaped at the plate, horror-struck.

"Uh-huh. Do you like it?"

Maybe this was all a bad dream. Aghast, she shook her head for a moment. Colin grinned, immensely pleased with himself. Only his action of pressing the keys into her hand finally galvanized her into speech.

"No." She threw them back as if they were red-hot. "Colin..." She put a hand to her brow, not even sure where to begin.

"What's the matter, Sabrina?" His smile faded as he began to look baffled. "Don't you like it? If you don't like the color, we can trade it in for—"

"No!" She took a deep breath to calm herself. "It's a terrific car. The color's fine." She stared helplessly at the expression on his young face, confusion vying with a heart-wrenching expectation of approval. "This is a very sweet gesture, but I can't accept it from you."

"Why not?" The excitement slowly died in his eyes.

No matter how much she hated to hurt his feelings, this had gone too far. It was vitally important that he understand, and there was only one way to do it.

"Colin . . . what you have for me is a schoolboy crush—nothing more, nothing less." She knew how much this would hurt him, but it had to be said. "One day you'll look back and wonder what you ever saw in me. . . ."

"That's not true!"

"To make any more of it than that is nonsensical." She persevered, keeping her tone as ruthlessly cool and matter-of-fact as she could make it.

He didn't reply for a moment, looking past her to stare fixedly down toward the lake as raw pain filled his eyes. She ached for him, but it had to be done this way.

Finally he said with quiet dignity, "I'll call the dealership and get them to come and pick up the car." She could hear the effort it took to keep his voice from quivering. He slid into the front seat of the Porsche and picked up the car phone.

Right now it didn't help to know that she'd tried everything else. Her heart ached for his wounded pride, and she worried about the damage to his fragile ego. But he would get over it, and probably sooner than he thought at the moment.

After a brief conversation he stepped partway out of the car and leaned an elbow on top of the open door. He refused to meet her eyes, except for a brief glance.

"The guy will be here this evening to pick it up, but they can't send anyone until after ten."

"Thank you," she murmured gently. "You know, it was a very sweet thought, even if I can't accept it."

Now he did meet her eyes. "I just thought it would make you happy."

He looked so hurt and dejected that she felt like comforting him with a hug, but instead she said softly, "Just being friends with you makes me happy."

He swallowed hard and his eyes were moist as he gave a wry little smile. "What did you have to go and say a thing like that for? Makes it hard for a guy to hate you."

A little relieved, she laughed softly, "I'm glad to hear that."

He stood there a moment longer, his expression strangely old on such a young face. "You're also a difficult person to love."

He got in and drove away, leaving her standing on the sidewalk looking after him. It was only when the black car turned onto busy Queen Street and finally disappeared that she walked up the steps.

She hated having to hurt him, remembering all too well how painful a teenage crush could be. Still, she had managed to survive her own adolescent traumas, and tried to cheer herself with the thought that Colin would, too.

SITTING ON THE TOP STEP of her front porch, Sabrina sank her chin on one hand and stared at the small, green car gleaming in the dusk. The sooner it was gone, the better.

From somewhere down the street came the sound of Edith Piaf's throaty voice. The scent of roses hung on the balmy evening air and a few houses down, beyond the boardwalk and the strip of beach, the newly risen moon hung swollen and golden over the lake.

But she couldn't even take any pleasure in the incredible beauty of the summer evening.

This whole business with Colin had left her with a heavy heart. He would get over it, but it worried her that he didn't have any close friends he could talk to, and he certainly wouldn't talk to Michael.

All this could only further complicate her feelings for his father, feelings she hadn't even got used to herself. Conflicting impulses and emotions spun crazily round and round in her brain until she felt overwhelmed and heaved a deep, dejected sigh.

Why did life have to be so complicated? No, *her* life had become complicated, in a way it had never been before. She gave another sigh and turned a little to lean back against the porch pillar.

Down the street on the nearly empty boardwalk a few couples strolled hand in hand, and beyond the beach the lake shimmered in the moonlight. She tried to let the peace of the evening calm her.

A car pulled up at the curb, the soft purr of the engine ceased, but she paid it little attention until the door slammed. Turning her head, she saw with a shock that it was Michael. Abruptly she stood up, helpless to keep the excitement from building inside as he walked toward her.

"Good evening, Sabrina."

He paused at the bottom of the path and looked up at her. Only the glow of the lamp in the living room window illuminated the dusky porch. His white shorts and T-shirt gleamed softly in the deep twilight.

"Michael...?" She felt suddenly uncertain as he remained silent. The smile of welcome died on her lips.

He ascended the steps until his face was level with hers and then she saw a hardness in his expression that made her stomach tighten into a painful knot.

"I apologize for this late visit but I needed to talk to you and I took a chance that you'd still be up." The chill formality in his voice made her shiver.

"Shall we go inside, then?"

As she began to turn away, he put a hand on her arm to stop her. The feeling of his strong, hard fingers on her skin made another kind of shiver go racing through her body.

"No. I can't stay long."

He could feel her trembling as she slowly turned toward him, and he quickly released her arm. Damn Colin. Damn this whole bloody situation.

She took a seat on the top step, clasped her hands between her knees and stared out at the street. He sank down beside her, all-too-aware of the heat of her body next to his, her delicate fragrance on the warm night air.

He wanted to take her in his arms, feel every inch of her soft body pressed against him once more. He wanted to carry her inside and make love to her and then he wanted to do it all over again and to hell with duty.

He gritted his teeth till his jaw ached. He had to forget this morning, forget how she made him feel.

"Sabrina, I want you to leave my son alone."

He spoke quietly, then turned to look at her, his face as implacable as granite.

"I'm afraid I'm putting this very bluntly, but try as I might, I couldn't think of any other way to say it." His remorseless gaze remained fixed on her. "I want you to end your association with Colin."

It wasn't that she didn't understand the flat, ruthless statement, but she couldn't quite prevent herself from echoing him. "My association?" Surely this was a bad dream and she'd soon wake up.

"Okay...your friendship." He spoke with impatience and stood up, dusting off his white shorts, every line of his lean body hard with tension and strain.

She rose to face him. "What's this all about, Michael?" She didn't mean to plead, but she couldn't believe they were having this conversation. "Look, if it's about the car..."

"It's not just the car," he burst out harshly, then stopped, as if searching for control. Moving a few paces away, he leaned on the porch railing to look out onto the street. "Even a little encouragement is all a teenage boy needs to—"

"Just a minute!" She stepped toward him, feeling the first traces of anger. "I haven't been encouraging Colin. You should know that."

He turned to look at her, stern and formidable—a stranger. Was this the man who had her trembling in his arms just a few hours ago?

"You say you're not encouraging him, but did you know Colin seems to feel that you need his help...?" He slammed his palm against the fluted pillar. "Dammit, his financial support!"

Anger gave way to confusion as she stared at him. "That's crazy!"

With a small, cold laugh he scanned her face, not a trace of warmth in his eyes. "It gets crazier. He has some idea that if he helps you out financially you'll care about him more." At her gasp of disbelief he looked away, shaking his head. "The kid's so naive, it scares me to death."

"I just don't understand where he got this idea that I need his financial support." Stunned and bewildered, she could only stare at him.

Now he looked at her with weary cynicism. "He wants to save you from your—how did he put it?—oh, yes . . ." He glanced back at the small house, in a look that encompassed her whole modest life-style. ". . . your poverty."

"Oh, no," she groaned.

"Did you know he raised the money for the car by selling the Rolex his grandmother gave him? And for a fraction of its value, I might add."

"How could I know that?" This had to be some kind of horrible nightmare. Her head was beginning to throb. She put a cold, trembling hand to her brow. "Is there any way of getting it back?"

"I'm sure there is, but I'm not going to bother. Obviously he isn't responsible enough to care for his belongings. Besides, I've never heard of anything so ridiculous as a seventeen-year-old with a fifty-thousand-dollar watch."

"You don't think I plan on *keeping* the car, do you?"

"No."

But the one terse word was not so much an acknowledgment of her good intentions, as a message that his will would prevail. He simply wouldn't allow her to keep it. But that wasn't what hurt so much. It was killing her that she actually had to defend herself.

He looked away toward the car, and stuffed his hands in his pockets. "If you don't get tough with him and this infatuation is allowed to continue unchecked, he'll want to keep on buying things to make life easier for you, and God knows what he'll buy next."

A wave of horror washed over her. "Wait a minute. What are you suggesting?" Her voice quivered and she had to will herself not to burst into tears.

"All I'm saying is, stop encouraging Colin in this ridiculous pursuit."

"I've never *encouraged* Colin," she said through clenched teeth. Through the pain, anger was beginning to boil in her veins. "As far as I'm concerned, we're just friends."

"It's not possible for you two to be friends." He turned his head at the sound of footsteps as a couple approached from the direction of the boardwalk. "Perhaps we should go inside to discuss this after all."

"No. Because there's nothing to discuss. Good night, Mr. Worth."

She turned away, yanked open the screen door and stepped into the house, but he was right behind her.

"Just a minute." He grabbed her arm, his grip strong and almost painful as he spun her around to face him in the small living room. "You can't just walk away. We're not through talking."

Her eyes filled with tears, but she'd be damned if she'd break down in front of him. "Oh, yes, we are."

She tried to wrench her arm out of his grasp, but he only took her other arm and pulled her even closer to his hard, unyielding body, so close that she could feel his heat burning into her cold flesh.

"You're taking this all wrong. I'm only doing this to protect my son."

"From me?"

He was so close, she had to tilt her chin to look up into his face. His fingers dug into her arms, and she watched his eyes darken in the heat of emotion.

"No, I'm the one who needs protection from you," he said with a groan, and pulled her to him, his lips coming down on hers.

She tried to push away, her hands trapped between them against his chest, but he only held her tighter, so that she could feel the length of his body burning into hers from breasts to hips. And then a hot wave of lethargy surged through her. She wanted that delicious pressure, needed him even closer.

Molding herself to him, she could feel his erection against her belly. Her knees gave way and she sagged against him. But his arms prevented her from falling, holding her tightly against his body, his hands sliding down her back to cup her hips.

He groaned breathlessly into her mouth. "Sabrina, I need you so much…."

Her fingers uncurled to caress the contours of his body. She felt his muscles clench and release at her touch. His lips stilled on hers and he went taut, dragging in deep ragged breaths that stopped abruptly as her fingertips traced over his belt buckle. Then she reached down and ran her fingers over the rigid length.

"Yes." He let out his breath in a convulsive gasp, "Yes," and pressed himself into her hand, his fingers kneading her buttocks, bringing her closer with small, deliberate, rhythmic movements.

Suddenly his grip tightened. "I can't stand this. I need to touch you." And before she knew what happened he stepped back and pulled her down with him onto the couch, onto his lap.

For a second she saw his eyes, a glittering blue staring down at her, hot, needful, and then his mouth took hers again, his hands feverishly pulling at her T-shirt. He was rigid beneath her and she squirmed in his lap, deliberately pressing her bottom against him, wanting to feel his hardness against her heat. He worked the shirt free and she felt cool air on her skin, felt his hands on her.

She looked down to see his lean, masculine fingers cupping her own small, firm breasts, his hand dark against her pale skin, and just the sight was so erotic that she felt a hot gush of moisture between her thighs.

"So beautiful," he whispered, his attention riveted on the swell of her breast, on the tightly budded dark crest.

He bent forward, his hungry mouth closed on her nipple and her head fell back with a gasp at the sudden onrush of sensation. She felt herself being carried away. What was she doing?

"No, Michael," she moaned, and tried to arch away from him. She couldn't let this go any further. They'd both regret it.

"Yes, Sabrina," he murmured, laving her nipple with his tongue.

She had to stop this—now.

"So, I'm good enough for you for sex, but not good enough to be friends with your son." She hardly recognized the frigid voice as her own. She quickly rolled off his lap, dragging down her shirt as she stepped away from him.

His head fell back and he squeezed his eyes shut, pressing his fingers against his closed eyelids. When he opened them again it was as if his face had been wiped clean of all expression, all hint of emotion.

Standing as tall as her shaking limbs would allow, her voice sounded cold and hollow. "Good night, Michael."

He got to his feet and looked at her a moment longer. A nerve flickered at the corner of his mouth, and his eyes filled with self-disgust. "Good night."

He turned and walked out, closing the door quietly behind him. She stood for a long time, just staring at the white-painted panels.

Finally she slumped onto the couch and cradled her head on her folded arms. She wouldn't be suffering like this if she hadn't fallen in love with Michael.

FOR THE NEXT THREE WEEKS she avoided both father and son and threw herself into work. Which wasn't difficult, because she'd been run off her feet organizing the back-to-school displays.

It hadn't been easy working around the ongoing construction. It was a nuisance for everyone, but Sabrina found it exciting to see her ideas taking solid form.

The boring old uniform aisles were now being broken up into self-contained boutique areas, starting right up front with Cosmetics, which was already completed. The counters were now set together in hexagonal wheels, and you could actually sit down on upholstered stools placed in front of mirrors with flattering lighting. Now the fluorescents were gone she could no longer jokingly refer to that area as the embalming center.

On a golden September afternoon, she sat at her desk for what seemed like the first time in days. Along with the display work, most of her week had been spent out at the warehouse, checking on the floats under construction. Almost every evening was occupied keeping up with work at the store. By the time she fell into bed, she was exhausted, which was a good thing. It left her no time to think about Michael.

He'd been away, first to Montreal, then Tokyo, then back to London again. He'd taken Anya with him and she saw it as just another demonstration of his thoughtfulness. He knew Anya and Perry had been keeping in touch, and it was almost as if he were giving them the opportunity to see each other. Obviously the fact that they were both employees made no difference to him in *this* case.

But she should be ashamed for being so petty when something good was happening for Anya. And it couldn't be easy maintaining a long-distance relationship. That one night with Perry had bloomed into something that made Anya blush every time his name was mentioned.

At least something was working out for somebody. But no matter how much it hurt, this was good for her. She knew now that she'd been nurturing a secret hope that something, some wonderful thing would happen between them. She'd been jolted back to reality, not once, but twice. Maybe this time the message would stick. He didn't trust her. Not with his son, and not with himself.

A knock sounded at the door and she called out absently, "Come in."

"Are you busy right now, Sabrina? Can I see you for a minute?"

She looked up from the fabric swatches in her hand to see Colin's face poking around the frosted glass door.

The few times she had run into him on the sales floor, his hurt withdrawal had been hard to take. There was little consolation in the thought that time healed all wounds. Michael had been right about the solution, but his methods left a lot to be desired.

"I have a lot of work to do right now, Colin. I'm afraid I don't have time to chat."

"This won't take long. Please, can't I just talk to you for a moment?"

He was so hesitant. The spark, the Worth confidence, had vanished. When she took a close look at him she felt alarmed. He was so solemn, not the cheeky, mischievous kid she knew. He would never be that kid again, she realized with a pang. A wave of love and caring for this boy swept over her. Michael's son.

"Well, just for a moment, then." She indicated the chair beside the desk.

He ignored the invitation and walked over to the window with jerky, agitated movements, to stand looking silently down onto the street below.

Sabrina swiveled her chair around and sat watching him. His fine-boned face looked drawn and there were dark smudges under his eyes—eyes so like his father's.

"I bet you're glad school's going to be starting next week," she said gently.

Colin turned to her wildly. "My father hates me, Sabrina."

She could only gasp in shock. "That's not true!"

He continued as if she hadn't spoken. "You don't know what it's like living with him."

There was nothing she could say. She could only watch helplessly as Colin frenetically paced the small office. Then he stopped and looked at her, and suddenly she saw a lost little boy and felt her heart turn over.

"Yesterday I went out to Grandma's grave. God, I miss her so much. I realize now how good she was to me, how kind, and I don't think I ever told her how much I loved her." He sank down into the chair on the other side of the desk, buried his face in his hands and began to sob. "I was such a stupid, selfish kid."

Swallowing hard, she sprang to her feet, went to him and put an arm around his heaving shoulders. "That's not true. She was very proud of you. You made her happy."

Suddenly he flung his arms around her waist and buried his face against her. "You don't know what it's like in that house now. You don't know how lonely it is. My father doesn't care about me. All he cares about is this damn store."

Another lump formed in her throat and she stroked the hair off his forehead. "No, Colin. That's not true. Your father loves you very much."

He shook his head. "I feel like I have nobody to care about what happens to me. Whether I live or die."

At his melodramatic declaration, a sad smile tugged at the corners of her mouth. But she felt stricken with guilt. Even she had let him down. This boy needed a friend. No matter what Michael thought, how could she turn her back on him?

"That's not true. I care."

"So this is where you are, Colin."

At the low, harsh sound of his voice she jerked upright to see Michael standing in the doorway, his eyes burning with anger, and something else. Something much more dangerous.

6

"I BELIEVE YOU HAVE work to do."

Michael gave Colin a cool, dismissive look and Sabrina felt anger welling up inside. Perhaps Colin hadn't been exaggerating about the climate at home.

"It's not fair to the people in your department for you to be wasting time."

At his father's words the boy's expression became sullen. It disturbed her to see his eyes filled with hatred as he rose to his feet.

"Thanks for listening, Sabrina," he said with shaky dignity.

"*Any*time, Colin."

As she spoke, she turned and shot Michael a defiant look. And yet, in spite of her anger, the sight of him caused a breathless ache in her heart. For the past three weeks, he'd never been out of her thoughts.

Colin walked out and Sabrina tensed as Michael stepped into her office, closed the door behind him with a small click and leaned back against it. His face was inscrutable.

The silence lengthened between them, until finally she put up a warning hand. "Before you say anything, I have something to say to you." He raised an eyebrow as she forged ahead. "Colin is suffering from a temporary infatuation. He'll get over it quicker if you don't make such a big deal out of it. In the meantime, he needs a friend. He depends on me to be that friend, and I'm not going to turn my back on him."

For a moment he said nothing; then, when he spoke, his voice was low and even. "Has it ever occurred to you that he could just be playing on your sympathy?" His small, cynical smile chilled her blood.

"What kind of a person are you? Your son was very upset, but you didn't even ask what the problem was. No wonder he thinks that you don't care about him."

"And what do *you* think?" Again his voice was low, but now it held an ominous note.

"It hardly matters what I think. Can't you see, he's still grieving for his loss? It's only been a matter of months since his grandmother died."

"I know exactly how long it's been."

"Then you should be a little more sympathetic."

The color drained from his face. "Thank you for your advice. Anything else?"

But she refused to be daunted by his cold sarcasm, even though her heart was breaking. "Now that you mention it, yes. I'm sure it's also frightening for him facing the fact that his childhood is over. And being aware of all the responsibilities he'll have to shoulder..."

"Thank you. I'm sure I would never have figured that out on my own."

His contempt cut her to the bone. But through the pain, anger flared. "Maybe if you were more approachable, instead of being such a...a...robot he *could* come to you with his problems."

He was already pale, but now his face set into a rigid mask, his voice low and strained with leashed anger. "If that's your opinion of me, I guess there's nothing more to be said, is there?"

She made sure her voice was as cold and clipped as his. "Except for one thing. Like I said before, Colin needs me. And I can't, and won't, turn my back on him."

Steadfastly, she held his icy gaze, refusing to let him intimidate her into backing down.

"So you're going to go against my explicit wishes?" Still he preserved the expressionless mask that gave nothing away.

Every muscle in her body tensed, striving to keep her emotions under strict control. "You're just going to have to trust me on this one."

"Need I remind you that Colin is a minor? And I still make his decisions for him, and if it has to be, that includes his choice of friends." His tone was almost conversational, but every line of his face was tightly etched with anger.

"What kind of a person do you think I am, that I would abandon a friend in need?"

He lunged away from the door, his impassivity suddenly gone and his eyes blazing. "For God's sake! You're ten years older than Colin."

"What does that have to do with anything?"

"What do you think he's looking for in a friendship like that?" His gaze traveled over her slowly before coming back to her eyes again. "Let me rephrase my question. What do *you* get out of it?"

The inference infuriated her so much that the words slipped out before she could stop them. "You're a bastard."

He stiffened. "You still haven't answered my question."

"Do I have to get something out of it?" All at once she couldn't stand it anymore and the anger gave way to weary desolation. He was impervious and she was so terribly vulnerable.

"Yes. In my experience everyone has their price."

"Don't judge me by your standards." She felt tears pricking at her eyes. "Now, if you don't mind, I have work to do. Provided I still have a job. Or does that depend on what you get out of *me?*"

His eyes held hers for a moment that seemed like an eternity. Then he turned abruptly and walked out of the office.

Sinking back against the desk, she covered her face with trembling hands, overwhelmed. What had she done?

SYBIL WORTH HAD once given a garden party for the employees, and Sabrina clearly remembered the grand old house. She gave the cabbie directions through the shady streets of Rosedale, past the mullioned windows and stone mansions of old-money Toronto.

She was probably crazy for going to his home, but she couldn't leave the accusation she had flung at him this afternoon hanging between them. Although she understood his fear for Colin, she had to make Michael see that he was asking something of her that her conscience said was wrong.

Most of all though, she bitterly regretted her criticism of him as a father. She *knew* how much he cared. She'd seen his attempts to do his best by Colin. His only crime was that in trying to protect his son, inexperience had made him clumsy.

Even so, why couldn't he see that she could be his ally in dealing with Colin? Instead, he had effectively rejected her friendship, and that was what hurt most deeply. But she had been totally wrong to use this issue to get back at him, even unconsciously.

The taxi dropped her at the open wrought-iron gates, just as a gleaming Cadillac turned into the drive. It pulled up a hundred feet ahead, in front of an imposing neo-Georgian facade ablaze with lights. A well-dressed couple emerged from the car as the front door opened and Michael himself appeared.

Sabrina stopped dead. He had company. What kind of stupid idea was this, going calling at the Worth mansion? She turned and began striding back down the drive.

"Sabrina?"

She walked a little faster.

"Sabrina, wait!"

She heard his footsteps crunching quickly down the gravel behind her and quickened her pace. Just as she reached the gate she felt a strong hand curl around her arm to stop her.

Her heart was pounding, but it wasn't from the exercise. Trying to calm herself, she slowly turned to face him.

"Sabrina." He stared down at her with a strange mixture of gladness and uncertainty that made her catch her breath. But he wasn't angry. It amazed her somehow.

"What are you doing here?" he asked softly.

He wore black tie and looked devastatingly handsome. She felt a sense of acute loss for what could never be, as sharp as any physical pain.

She cleared her throat. "I wanted to talk to you, but I shouldn't have come. I can see you're busy. Perhaps some other time." Turning quickly, she began to walk away again.

Once more he stopped her, this time with both hands on her arms, his fingers gently massaging her flesh with intoxicating pressure, so close behind her that she could feel his warm breath on her hair.

"Please, don't go yet." His low murmur made the very air around her vibrate with suppressed emotion. "Not till you've given me a chance to apologize for this afternoon."

There was something in his voice she'd never heard before, something that caused her breathing to become rapid and shallow.

Slowly he turned her around to face him. And there was something new in his eyes—a bright intensity.

He looked into her eyes and she saw self-condemnation. "Sabrina, I'm sorry. Can you ever forgive me?"

Somehow he had hold of her hands and his fingers were absently playing with hers. He searched her face anxiously, his voice rueful, yet resigned. "I don't understand why I'm behaving like such a jerk."

She pulled her hands away from him. His warm, caressing fingers were making a mockery of her concentration.

"I'm the one who should apologize. I said some unforgivable things and I would do anything in the world to take them back."

"What did you say that wasn't true?"

He moved to close the distance and her senses swam again with his nearness, feeling the warmth of his body on her skin as if they were actually touching.

"What I said was cruel and wrong. I had no right to sit in judgment." Emotion tightened her throat, making her voice husky.

He moved slowly until he stood on the other side of the gate, looking at her through the scrollwork, and she couldn't avoid his gaze. He stared down into her eyes as if he wanted to probe the secrets of her soul. Suddenly aware of the deep silence, she caught her breath.

They stood quite alone by the big iron gates. The towering oaks and maples lining the street were disappearing into an evening mist that softened the outlines of the great house behind him, and she could see droplets of moisture swirling in the soft nimbus of light around the gatepost carriage lamps.

Once again she felt deeply, dangerously vulnerable. Michael had a power over her, a sexual magnetism that could make her forget everything. She had to get away from him, because it was only away from him that she could deal with the feelings he aroused in her.

"That's all I have to say." She choked out the words. "I'll let you get back to your guests now. Good night."

She spun away, but he moved quickly around the gate and stepped in front of her, barring her escape.

He took her hands. "No, please. Don't go," he finished softly, yet with what might have been a hint of pleading.

She could only stare up at him, too astounded to say anything. Then suddenly her eyes filled with tears and his face fragmented in front of her. Willing them not to spill over onto her cheek, she determinedly blinked them away. But she couldn't stop her voice from quivering, or the words from tumbling out.

"I was foolish enough to think you knew me better than to have such a low opinion of me."

"I don't have a low opinion of you. I have a low opinion of me."

With a shake of her head, she pulled her hands away from his and took a deep breath. "Before you go any further, I want you to know that I didn't just come to apologize. Regardless of what you think, I meant what I said this afternoon. I'm not going to turn my back on Colin. He needs me."

"My son is very lucky to have someone like you on his side." He shoved his hands into his pockets and raised his face to the misty lamplight. Taking a deep breath, he looked down at her again, and now there was derision in his face. "I was jealous." He gave a small mocking laugh. "Of my own son."

She expelled her breath sharply. "What are you saying?"

"Pretty depraved stuff, huh?" He gave another brief, humorless laugh, holding her in his intense, ironic gaze.

"Oh, Michael, I'm not trying to take your son away from you."

He took both her arms in a painful grip and brought her around to face him. "No!" he ground out, then repeated, low and tense, "I was jealous of Colin."

"You mean..." She finally understood what he was trying to say. Slowly she shook her head and stepped away from him. "No, you can't mean that."

He smiled with a self-mocking twist of the lips. "I'm afraid I do." His eyes gleaming with breathtaking intensity, he slowly stepped toward her. "I think we need to talk."

Her knees shook as she backed away from him, holding out one hand to ward him off, but she was weakening—she could feel it. Finally she felt the rough brick of the gatepost against her back.

His unrelenting gaze held hers as he reached out and cupped her face in his hand. She closed her eyes as his thumb slowly slid across her cheek with a soft, featherlight touch that left her skin tingling.

But when it slid caressingly over her parted lips and insinuated itself between them, her lids flew open. For a moment she stared into his glittering eyes, more intensely blue than she had ever seen them before, even in the shadowed light.

He held her mesmerized, as if he were drinking in the sight of her. Then, with a small, anguished sigh, he slowly lowered his head and she held her breath until his lips settled on hers.

A warm, tender and searching kiss at first, it quickly became hot and demanding. She fought the urge to wrap her arms around him, but couldn't stop herself from clinging to his lapels, trembling so hard, she was afraid she couldn't hold herself up. When his tongue parted her lips for a few insane moments she reveled in the sensual delight, the arousal that left her quivering with the need for more.

Instead she turned away and pushed gently at his chest. He released her, but placed one arm on either side of her, keeping her prisoner.

"Michael... I have to go now."

"Sabrina..."

"No." She pushed his arm and he dropped it, freeing her so she could put some distance between them. He remained standing by the gatepost, his gaze holding hers with unwavering intensity. "This is still crazy."

"Yes, I know," he murmured, "but there's no denying it's happening."

She turned and looked at the house, blazing with lights. The mansion stood as a tangible symbol of all the reasons why this would never work.

"No. I can't deny it. But you said yourself that you had no time for involvements. You said your work consumed you."

"Ever since I met you, work seems to be the farthest thing from my mind." He gave her a rueful smile.

She shook her head. "You said—"

"Sabrina, I said a lot of stupid things. All I know is that something's happening between us and I want to find out what it is."

"Whatever may or may not be happening between us, *I* don't want it to go any further." She was amazed at how steady and decisive her voice sounded.

He betrayed no reaction, then sighed and gave a small shrug. "Then I have to respect your wishes, don't I?"

"Yes," she murmured. "Good night."

She turned on trembling legs toward the road, but he reached out and stopped her, cupping her shoulder with his warm, lean fingers.

"Wait a minute. How did you get here?"

"I took a cab."

"Well, then, you'd better come inside while I call one for you."

"That won't be necessary. I can flag one down when I get to Bloor Street."

"If you think I'm going to let you roam around looking for a cab at this time of night, you can think again."

"Really. . . I'll be fine."

"Sabrina, don't argue with me."

His tone told her there'd be no point. Reluctantly she walked with him up the gravel drive lined with flower beds and shrubbery to the house. Passing through the pillared portico, he opened one of the main double doors to usher her in. She hung back, but he gave her a push.

"Don't just stand there, go on in."

The foyer was a vast expanse of black-and-white marble tiles leading to a broad red-carpeted staircase. In the center of the hall stood a beautifully carved antique Queen Anne table polished to a mirrorlike finish, reflecting a silver bowl of roses.

Three sets of doors opened off each side of the staircase. Through the nearest doors to her right she could hear voices and laughter. Michael took her elbow and led her toward the sounds.

"No." She jerked violently away from him.

"What's wrong?" He looked taken aback.

"I don't want to go in there."

"Why not? You can meet my friends, maybe have a drink while you wait for your cab."

"No," she said firmly. At his puzzled look she added, "I'm not dressed."

He let his eyes drop slowly over her white T-shirt, lingering on the outline of her breasts before going on to her worn and faded jeans, then gave her a small, dangerous smile that made her toes curl. "You look fine to me."

She couldn't allow herself to be distracted. "Really, I'd rather not."

He shrugged. "Okay, then you'd better come in here." His smile became even more dangerous. "At least I'll have you all to myself for a few minutes more."

Linking his long fingers with hers, he led her across the hall to the opposite front corner room that seemed to be his study. In the soft glow of the green-shaded lamp on the desk, she could see one wall lined with books from floor to ceiling. An overstuffed leather sofa and two armchairs were set on a Persian carpet in front of the fireplace, and the tall, elegant Georgian windows filling the two remaining walls looked out onto the misty drive.

Michael stepped over to pick up the phone, resting one hip on the desk, while she hovered indecisively by the door.

"Don't just stand there. I'm not going to bite you. Come in and sit down." With a smile, he hooked one foot around the leg of a Duncan Phyfe chair and pulled it nearer the desk.

As he ordered the cab, she sank down unwillingly into the chair and looked around the room, anywhere but at his face.

He hung up. "It'll be here soon."

"Good." She realized how much relief there had been in that one word. "I mean, I feel terrible keeping you from your guests like this."

He still had that small disturbing smile, as if he could see through her lame excuses and knew exactly why she was nervous. The hint of satisfaction made her feel wary.

"I'm sure they can entertain themselves for a few minutes." The smile deepened. "This evening has turned out a lot better than I had anticipated."

At that moment headlights swung across the room from the drive outside. Sabrina breathed a sigh of relief and stood up. But he stood at the same time and they were suddenly much too close.

"My cab's here," she murmured inanely, looking up into his eyes, intense, penetrating, waiting. *To hell with reason,* desire murmured urgently. All she had to do was take one step closer and press her yearning body against his.

"Sabrina, do you want to send him away?" His voice was a husky whisper. "Do you want me to send them *all* away?"

She backed up, tripping over the chair behind her. He reached out to steady her, bringing her close against him.

"You're crazy." She let out a nervous, breathless little laugh. "You'd do that for me?" The thought of him sending his distinguished guests packing just because he wanted to be with her was ludicrous.

But he cupped his hand under her chin. "I'd rather be with you than anyone else." The simple, unequivocal sincerity in his voice left her defenseless.

"Michael..." In his eyes she saw blazing desire, the same desire burning up the air between them.

He was going to kiss her. She felt a sense of panic rising up inside. If he touched her, if his lips touched hers, it would be disastrous, irrevocable. They would be making love, blind to his friends waiting across the hall, blind to the cab waiting outside. None of that would matter. She'd be lost to all reason except her need for him.

She put a hand on his chest to stop him. "Please...I have to go."

He sighed and looked down into the slightly pleading expression in her eyes. For a moment he tightened his grip. He wanted her so badly right now. He wanted to carry her upstairs and make love to her, because making love to her would drive away the loneliness, the depressing memories this house held for him.

But she didn't want that to happen and he had to respect that. He could see that she was fighting the attraction. It would be easy to seduce her. And unless she wanted him as much as he wanted her right now, it would a cold kind of comfort.

He slowly released her and she took a hasty step back. "Goodbye, Michael."

In one desperate rush, she fled the room, raced across the foyer and out through the front door. That should tell him all too clearly that she didn't want any kind of involvement with him. Did he need to be hit over the head to make it sink in?

SABRINA SAT beside Charlie on a bench on the Beaches boardwalk in the shade of a big old willow, looking out on the dark blue expanse of Lake Ontario. She'd put it off until now so it wouldn't spoil their dinner, but he deserved to know. And after walking around half the day, stunned and bitter, she needed to talk.

"Charlie, I have something important to tell you."

He turned and gave her a long look, his eyes twinkling. "Is it time to wish you happy?"

For a second she stared at him in confusion, then realized what he was getting at and blushed scarlet. Charlie gave her a keen, probing look.

"Michael Worth is canceling the parade," she said quickly. "This year will be the last."

His face fell, but she sensed that his disappointment had nothing to do with the parade. "That's too bad. I'm really sorry to hear that." Charlie shook his white head, only mildly regretful. "It'll be missed."

"Bad! It's devastating! How could he do this to me?" She saw him shoot her a questioning look and added, "I mean . . . to make a decision like this without even telling me."

"If he didn't tell you, then how do you know?"

"I overheard Walter Stevenson talking to Jonathan." That was the worst of it. Sitting there in her office, hearing them out in the corridor solemnly agreeing that it was the end of an era. "And when I asked Anya, she didn't deny it."

"I see." Charlie stroked his chin thoughtfully. "This won't affect your job, Sabrina. After all, it's not just the parade . . ."

"I'm not worried about my job. But if he cancels the parade it'll the first time in seventy years that Toronto hasn't had one. Think about the kids, Charlie! And the memories it brings back for their parents and grandparents. Nothing brings people together in this city like that parade. The bigger Toronto gets, the more we need it. There are so few occasions when we remember that we're all neighbors and feel a sense of community."

"Yes, I know, Sabrina. . . ." He nodded patiently.

"And what about the volunteers? People like you."

"I know, Sabrina. . . ."

"Think of old George. He's been marching in that parade since he was a Boy Scout."

"I know, Sabrina . . ."

"For the past five years he's been doing a terrific job of coordinating the marching bands. He does it for nothing. It's part of his life."

"Sabrina," Charlie broke in finally. "Why don't you go to Michael Worth and talk to him about it?"

"That's exactly what I'm going to do. He's coming home from London tonight."

Charlie shifted a little on the bench and fixed her with a serious look. "Now, Sabrina, don't you go flying off the handle and say or do something you'll regret. Maybe you'd better wait until Monday morning to have this little chat."

"And spend a whole weekend wondering what's going on? Uh-uh." She shook her head emphatically.

"Is that the only reason you want to go over there tonight?"

She turned away from the probing look in his eyes and stared out at a freighter on the lake. "What other reason could there be?"

SHE WAITED until she saw the limo turn in through the gates, then hurriedly paid off the taxi driver and got out of the cab. As she began walking up the dark drive, Michael emerged from the long black car. Her heart constricted painfully and her breathing began to speed up. Who was she kidding? She couldn't care less about the parade right now, she just wanted to see Michael again.

Hardly realizing she'd done it, she called out to him softly. Her voice gave away too much. It sounded husky and tinged with longing.

He turned his head quickly, and when he saw her, there was no mistaking the surprise, then the happiness in the smile lighting his face. He began walking down the drive toward her, suit jacket flapping open with his long, fluid stride, accentuating his lean body.

She reveled in the thrilling knowledge that her presence brought him pleasure.

Tires squealed somewhere behind her as the glare of headlights swept across Michael's face. She turned in horror to see a car roaring in through the gates, only a few feet away.

Without another conscious thought, she leapt to one side, instinctively putting up her arms to shield her face and landing hard in a clump of bushes.

In the confusion of the next few seconds she felt the rough, sharp branches digging painfully into her bare skin, heard Michael yelling out her name, his voice sharp with fear as the headlights sliced past and the car swerved off to the right, tearing up the gravel as it skidded to a stop.

Sudden, abrupt silence fell.

Dazedly aware of a million painful pokes and prickles, Sabrina struggled to lift her face from the protective cradle of her arms and disentangle her legs from the shrubbery. A car door slammed and then she heard Colin's voice, high-pitched with fright.

"Sabrina, where are you?"

But Michael reached her first as she tried to turn over and sit up. "Darling, are you all right?" He sank down on his knees beside her.

His anxious voice shook with terror and his hands were trembling as they slid underneath her. She must be really dazed. Had he called her darling?

As he carried her out of the bushes she bit back a wince at the twigs scratching her bare arms. He placed her gently on the narrow grass verge bordering the drive and cradled her close. She could feel him shaking as he smoothed the hair away from her brow.

"I'm fine. Really, I'm fine." She could have stayed in his arms all evening, but for the sight of Colin's ashen face leaning over her and the terror in his eyes.

"Honest to God, Sabrina, I didn't see you." His voice sounded thick and hoarse, as if he were about to burst into tears. She could smell the unmistakable odor of alcohol.

"It's all right, Colin." She struggled to a sitting position and would have stood up to show him that she wasn't badly hurt, but Michael wouldn't let her. He held her tighter with one arm as the other hand ran over her body, apparently checking for injuries.

"He didn't hit you, did he?"

"No, he didn't hit me. I'm just winded from landing in the bush. If you'll let me get to my feet, I'll be fine."

Colin let out a groan of relief and jumped forward to help her up. Michael rose as she did, keeping a supporting arm around her. As she gained her feet, a wave of dizziness made her sway a little and clutch at Michael's arm. Only then did she notice the horrified chauffeur standing in the middle of the drive.

She stepped away from Michael and began shakily wiping off bits of brush and dirt.

"You see, I really am all right." She gave them both a tremulous smile, intensely uncomfortable at being the center of all this attention.

Michael seemed unconvinced. He looked down at her with a worried frown.

"Thank God." Colin sighed in heartfelt relief.

His father turned on him savagely. "And so you damn well should. Do you realize you could have killed her?"

Sabrina let out a cry and Colin flinched in shock.

"Of course I do." This time his defiance was tinged with fear and he stammered a little. "But...but how was I supposed to know someone would be walking on our driveway at this time of night?"

"That's besides the point. I've warned you about your driving before. And you've been drinking tonight, haven't you?" Michael looked like a man at the end of his rope. "Hand me your keys."

"You can't do that to me." Colin's voice rose until it squeaked with anger. "You can't treat me like a kid."

"Don't tell me how I can treat you," Michael ground out. "I've tried to be patient...."

"You mean apathetic, don't you? You don't give a damn about me. Don't start pretending that you do."

At the venom in his son's words, Michael's face went dead white and his voice dropped to a deceptive quiet. "Colin, go to your room."

The boy laughed hysterically. "Do you think you're talking to a twelve-year-old? You can't just send me to my room. That's the way it's always been, right? Send me away when you don't want to listen to the truth."

"The truth is that you're a spoiled brat. I don't know what your grandmother—"

"Don't you talk about my grandmother! At least she cared. I hate you," Colin screamed as he threw the keys at his father. "I wish you were dead!"

7

RIGID WITH TENSION, Michael stood watching his son run into the house, then he looked down at the keys in his hand.

He tossed them to his driver, who stood staring at him anxiously. "Could you put his car away, please." He turned slowly toward her. The lines were etched a little deeper on his face, and he looked exhausted.

Sabrina walked over and wrapped her arms around him, her heart bursting with tenderness and compassion and love. How she longed to take his pain away.

After a tiny moment of hesitation, his arms closed around her, gathering her tightly to him. She could feel the trembling in his strong limbs and knew right now he needed *her*.

The sound of a car door softly shutting and being driven away seemed to bring him to awareness. Stepping away from her, Michael looked down into her face.

After a long, searching look, a slow smile curved his lips, banishing the bleakness from his eyes. "You're very sweet," he whispered, pressing his lips against her forehead in the lightest of kisses.

Then he put her gently from him and took her hand, examining the long scratch on her forearm. "We should do something about this before it gets infected."

"I'm sure it'll be fine."

In answer he only shook his head and started toward the house, pulling her along with him. "I'm sure it will be, as soon we get some antiseptic on it."

Opening the front door, he led her inside, but she pulled back. "No, Michael. I can do that at home. You're wiped. I should just get out of here and let you get some rest."

With a sudden surge of desperation, he squeezed her hand more tightly. He couldn't bear the thought of her leaving him here alone.

"No," he said quietly. "Don't go yet. Please. I need to assure myself that you're really all right."

The foyer was dark and silent, except for a small lamp burning on the hall table. Colin must be in his room, the housekeeper long gone to her coach house, and as soon as the cars were locked up, Fred would retire to his apartment above the garage. The big house stood almost empty, peopled by the ghosts of unhappy memories.

He led her toward the staircase, but she resisted.

"No, Michael, this is silly!"

"Maybe. But I don't really want to be by myself right now."

She was very close and he was painfully aware of how alone they were. They could be the only people on earth. He *wished* that they were, that it could be as simple as that.

"I don't think that would be a good idea."

"It would be a terrible idea, but stay anyway, please." He couldn't believe he was reduced to pleading, but this need was so powerful, it would be so easy to lose himself in it, forget everything else, if only for tonight.

"It's late. I really should go."

Even though she quickly turned away, he could see the longing flaring in her eyes. He *should* let her go, but tonight, God help him, he hadn't the strength to play the hero. She was so warm and soft and strong, and he needed her. Needed her caring, needed her tenderness. He stopped her by capturing her hand again, twining his fingers in hers, feeling her response in the tightening of her grip.

"At least let me look after your scrapes and bruises." Sabrina opened her mouth to speak, but he held up a hand, his voice soft and huskily persuasive. "It's the least I can do, and it would make me feel so much better."

The slow trembling inside her began to spread, yet she allowed him to lead her upstairs and along a corridor toward the white painted double doors at the other end. She could no more resist him than stop breathing.

The passage was lit only by a single lamp on a small, delicately carved antique table. Alone in this big, quiet house, their footsteps made only the faintest brush on the carpet running down the center of the polished oak floor.

He opened the door and stood aside for her to pass. She stepped in, then stopped at the view that met her eyes.

The room lay in darkness. But a large, uncurtained bow window opened to the fragrant night air. Beyond the dense black mass of trees in the foreground rose the glittering city skyline, dominated by the spire of the CN Tower.

His hands closed over her shoulders as he moved her forward. Then he closed the door and flicked a switch. The glow of a floor lamp revealed a comfortable sitting room.

"Why don't you take a seat and I'll be with you in a moment." He walked over to her left and opened a sliding door set into the white wainscotted paneling. Through the doorway she could see a bed, with a white duvet turned down in the soft light of a bedside lamp. His bedroom?

She had no business here. She should leave, and yet she walked over to the window and sank down to her knees on the upholstered window seat to look out at the skyline. Lord knows, she really should leave, but she yearned so much to just be with him.

"Okay, we're all set."

At the sound of his husky voice she spun around to see him holding a small box in one hand and a bowl in the other.

"Michael, I should be going." Her voice emerged in a broken, throaty gasp. He affected her too deeply, so just being here became a risk.

"And you will, as soon as I get these seen to. Now sit down." He put the box and bowl on the window seat, took her arms and firmly but gently sat her down.

He sank to his knees in front of her with a smile, then took her arm in his hand. She flinched as his warm fingers closed around her.

"Sorry."

He'd come nowhere near the scratches. Merely his gentle touch sent shivers rippling down every nerve.

All at once she realized that her arms had been hurting the whole time.

He began to dab at the largest scrape on her forearm.

"Ouch!" she yelped, in response to the searing sting of the antiseptic.

"Hold still."

She turned to see his glossy dark head bent over her arm, his lean fingers firmly curved around her wrist, and the pain was swept aside by the shudder of desire storming through her. She had to clench her teeth and try to get the feeling under control. *Do something, say something,* anything to distract herself.

"It's such a nice view from this window."

"It's even nicer during the day when you can see the ravine." He kept his eyes on his task, dabbing at her arm with the antiseptic-soaked cotton, but the sound of his low, resonant voice sent a tingle up her spine.

Glancing around, she took in the overstuffed, comfortable furniture, the wall full of books, the stereo in one corner and the wood-mantel fireplace. In a house of cold perfection, this room was warm and cosy and welcoming.

"I could spend my life in a room like this."

He stopped cleaning the wound and went very still.

Suddenly she realized what she had said and hurried on. "I mean...you've got books, music and a view.... That's all it takes to make me happy." She tried to sound flippant, but her laughter had the nervous edge of fear.

In the pressing need to distract herself, she hardly knew what she was saying. He wanted her, but he would never force himself on her—she knew that instinctively. No, it was herself she was afraid of. Her response to him, her unbridled desire.

He lifted his eyes to hers and she trembled under his quiet, searching gaze. Was he trying to read her secret? But he simply smiled, as if to reassure her, then looked back down to resume tending her arm.

Unobserved, she examined his face. Even when he was smiling, there always seemed to be something melancholy deep down inside, something that seemingly couldn't be erased, that struck a chord with her. What a sad life he'd endured. His poor relationship with his mother, a brief, doomed marriage, the tragedy of his wife's death and now all his troubles with Colin. Suddenly she needed to know everything about him.

"Why did Colin have to live with his grandmother?"

He stopped stroking the cotton over her skin and looked up at her in surprise.

"I'm sorry," she said quickly. "That's none of my business—"

"He didn't have to stay with his grandmother," he cut in. "He chose to live with her. I'm sure you've noticed my son's unequivocal dislike of me."

His dispassionate tone made it even more shocking than if he'd blurted out the words in distress. As if he had long since taken the pain for granted and never expected it to change.

"I know how much that must hurt you. I know how much you love Colin."

He screwed the cap back on the antiseptic, put it in the box and threw away the used cotton in a wastebasket under the small escritoire behind him.

Finally he sank back on his heels and looked at her, his face an emotionless mask. "How do you know that?"

She shrugged. "Woman's intuition."

"If that woman's intuition is leading you to feel sorry for me, don't. The truth is, I did put him in Sybil's care when I should have tried to make a go of it on my own. And I deserve what I got." His bluntness made it only too clear that, once again, he didn't want her pity.

But she couldn't, and wouldn't, believe him to be so self-serving. He simply wasn't a man she could ever think capable of being as cruel and callous as he was making himself out to be.

"You must have been very young, and left on your own with a tiny baby!" She could picture all too easily how lost and anxious she would have felt in his position. She would turn to her parents. It was only natural. "You were only trying to do the best for Colin. You shouldn't blame yourself."

"How do you know that?"

"Because I know you."

He sighed loudly. "My son resents me today because, for all intents and purposes, I walked away from him." She started to speak, but he cut her off. "No! Don't try to excuse me. I did what I did."

No matter how hard he tried, he couldn't talk her into thinking badly of him. "Colin told me you were always around—messing up his life, as he put it." She shrugged and gave an apologetic smile. "It doesn't sound to me as if you abandoned him."

"That's obviously not the way Colin sees it."

"Why didn't you have him come and live with you when he was older?" She already knew Michael to be incapable of dishonorable behavior. She didn't need to exonerate him, but she wanted to *know* him, to understand him.

"I tried. By the time Colin was four, I could finally afford a suitable home for him. Up to that point I'd been living in digs, which even in those days cost me practically everything I earned."

"Where were your digs? Buckingham Palace?" After all, he was still a Worth.

He gave her a reluctant smile. "I suppose it's natural you'd assume I had the same kind of cash flow Colin enjoys, but I had to live on my salary, and in those early years, it didn't amount to much."

"Couldn't your mother have helped you?"

He gave a dry chuckle. "Sybil was afraid I took after my father too much. That was her way of ensuring I developed a backbone."

She felt a wave of resentment and anger at Sybil's shabby treatment of her son. She had the resources to help Michael, but she didn't seem to have done anything except take his son away from him. "So what happened when he was four?"

"Sybil talked me out of taking him, said he was happy, that it would be cruel to drag him away from the only home he'd ever known."

"You could have transferred to the Toronto store."

"I tried. But she wanted me in London. And after all, she was the boss."

"But what about Colin? How did he feel about it?"

"I was almost a stranger to him. One trip a year, at Christmas, was all I could afford back then. Hardly enough to establish a relationship...."

It was hard not to think of how Sybil had indulged Colin. The Porsche, the Rolex, membership in the exclusive Royal Canadian Yacht Club. Not to mention the frequent trips to some of the most famous resorts the world had to offer. She couldn't believe the disparity. Was that his mother's way of punishing Michael for marrying against her wishes?

"Sybil made frequent trips across the Atlantic, but she never brought Colin. We battled about it constantly. She never failed to remind me of the obligation I was under." His face hardened and she could hear the latent anger in his voice. "After all, she was doing me a favor. I was being selfish and ungrateful."

She knew it must be an echo of Sybil's words. "For wanting to see your son?"

"When it was so inconvenient and cruel to the child," he continued in bitter mockery. "There was always an excuse. He didn't travel well. He was teething. His nursery school program couldn't be interrupted."

Pathetically flimsy excuses to keep father and child apart, when Sybil should have been doing all in her considerable power to keep them together. "That was a terrible thing for her to do."

"On the contrary, she did help me out by taking care of Colin in the first place." His lips hardened, the skin around his mouth white with tension. She knew there was much more he wasn't telling her and no reason why he should.

"So that was it? Colin lived with his grandmother from that point on?"

He shook his head. "In effect. By then, of course, I was making more money and traveling more for Worth's. I spent more time over here. I saw Colin on a regular basis. But he always clung to his grandmother and shied away from me. I'm not quite sure when, or why, the resentment kicked in."

She felt a bitter pang of sympathy. "Oh, Michael..."

"When he was twelve I decided he was old enough to make the move to England. I felt it was time Colin and I established a more normal relationship. And besides, at that point, whether he agreed or not, Colin needed... a firmer hand."

That, she could well imagine. "So what happened?"

"It lasted about eight months. By the time he'd been kicked out of his third school, I knew I was fighting a losing battle. The boy simply did not want to be with me."

"And now?"

"And now it's too late. I can't change the way Colin feels about me, but I also realize that now, more than ever, he needs me. I just wish I could be sure I'm doing the right thing."

Michael was always so much in control—of his emotions, his world. And now for the first time she was seeing him unsure of himself.

"The important thing you have to remember is that you love Colin and you're trying your best." The words sounded so trite. She felt a galling sense of impotence at her inability to offer anything more.

He raised his eyes to hers, brilliant with moisture, and the sight went straight to her heart. Suddenly she was painfully aware of the quiet.

Michael got up from his knees abruptly. "I'll just get rid of these." He picked up the bowl and box and went back through the sliding door.

Churned-up and jittery, she got to her feet. She'd stayed here far too long.

As he came back into the room his eyes met hers again and she had difficulty catching her breath. "It's late." She glanced at her watch, then back up to him, trying to keep the smile on her face casual and noncommittal. "You look like you could use a good night's sleep. I'll see you Monday."

Without taking his eyes from hers, he slowly walked closer until he was only a foot away.

"Please don't go." She heard the ache of loneliness.

Her heart began to pound. For the first time she realized how powerful and how destructive love could be. For this was truly love. Not just a dreamy fantasy, but the need to share everything, both the passion and the pain.

"I *have* to go."

Her whisper fell into the silence. Charged silence. Something dark and intense shadowed his eyes as they searched hers, and she was suddenly afraid that he would see too much, right down into her secret heart, to the truth of her love for him.

"I have to go," she repeated.

And yet she couldn't tear herself away from that look in his eyes, couldn't force her feet to move toward the door. And when he took another step closer she couldn't move from the spot.

"Sabrina," he murmured in a low, husky whisper. "Please stay."

"Oh, Michael, we're making a big mistake." Her breathless voice shook as he reached out and cupped her face in his strong, lean fingers.

She slowly put a trembling hand against his cheek, feeling the slight roughness of stubble. He turned his face and gently pressed a kiss into her palm with firm, hot lips.

One kiss, just one kiss. Surely she could afford that much. With a small moan, she moved against him, suddenly consumed by the hunger to feel him, to have his arms about her, to know the pressure of his heated flesh against her body.

His mouth ground against hers. He parted her lips with almost brutal intensity. A tormented moan escaped her as she strained closer, clutching the hair at his nape with her fingers, unable to get close enough.

With a groan he lifted her off her feet. His strong arms wrapped around her tightly, molding her to the length of his body. One hand cupped her buttocks and pressed her closer as she wrapped her legs around him. His erection ground against her pelvis. She rocked rhythmically against him. This feeling was too intense, almost frightening.

"Please let me go. Don't make me do this."

He murmured against her mouth. "You're free to walk out of here any time you want." But his lips were hot and persuasive.

She groaned with frustration. She could no more walk out of here than she could sprout wings and fly. Her mouth opened wider to his, greedy and desperate for more as his tongue entwined and retreated and teased her, driving her wild.

He pulled away a fraction. "You've had your chance to escape. It's too late."

She pressed herself even more tightly against him. "I'd rather die of ecstasy than frustration."

A shaky laugh escaped him. "Your wish is my command."

And then his mouth found hers again and without breaking the kiss he set her down and began unbuckling her belt and pushed her jeans down over her hips.

She did the same for him and looked down to see his erection straining the white cotton underwear. She reached down to cup her hand around him.

He let out a sharp hiss. "Can we go someplace a little more comfortable?"

Her voice was a shaky whisper against his mouth. "What's wrong with the carpet? I can't wait a second longer."

She felt a shudder go through him as he sank to his knees and laid her down on the floor, straddling her. He leaned over and captured one tightly aching nipple in his mouth, hot and wet through the cotton T-shirt. She arched against him in feverish pleasure, desperate to feel his devastating assault on her naked flesh.

She pulled at her shirt and he lifted his head, allowing her to drag it upward. He sharply drew in his breath as his gaze ran over her.

Slowly, excruciatingly slowly, he lowered his head again and she felt an avalanche of sensation as his mouth closed over one nipple. Fingers trembling, she began unbuttoning his shirt, desperate to feel his skin against hers. Running her hands over the smooth golden flesh of his torso, she gave a soft moan of pleasure as he moved to her other breast, now sensuously suckling, now biting down gently on the hardened peak until she burned at fever pitch. She wanted him now.

She slid her hand lower over his stomach, to slip beneath the waistband of his underwear until her fingers closed around him, his skin hot and hard.

He sucked in his breath with a shudder. "Now you've gone and done it."

She gave a throaty laugh, feeling bold and triumphant in her feminine power. "Done what?" she teased.

"Pushed me past the point of no return, lady." He grinned, and that damned dimple appeared.

Her gaze ran over his long, lean body, over the smooth muscles that rippled down his stomach to his erection. He was so beautiful, he took her breath away. The naked heat in his eyes as he looked back at her made her hunger grow by leaps and bounds.

"Promises, promises..." she groaned as she reached for him, not even able to wait those few milliseconds before she could touch him again. She wanted to take him into her mouth, caress him with her tongue, taste the very essence of him.

He nuzzled her lips, his breath warm and rapid, as she could feel him hard and ready, nudging against her. She couldn't wait to feel him inside her, to take him into the sanctuary of her body, to keep him safe with her love and bring him pleasure.

"I'm sorry, love, but I can't wait another moment." He sighed into her mouth, sheathing himself deep inside her with one powerful movement.

"Oh, Michael," she moaned.

"Shhh..." He soothed her, pushing the damp tendrils of hair off her brow with one trembling hand, his breathing labored as he covered her face with small, tender kisses. "Take it easy, darling. I don't want to hurt you."

The momentary discomfort had faded, and now all she wanted was to feel him moving inside her. She rocked her hips enticingly against him. Even the slightest movement added to the building throbbing heat. He shuddered and began to thrust rhythmically into her.

The sound of her name on his lips was incredibly arousing. She pulled his head back to hers and took his mouth in a drugging kiss, as his right hand massaged one breast, teasing the aching nipple. His body convulsed and then finally the pressure tightening inside her exploded in an intense, shuddering climax.

She murmured, "Michael, I love..." and caught herself just in time. "...what you do to me."

Looking down at her, his hair damp and ruffled, his chest heaving, Michael's face lit up with that devilish grin and her heart expanded with love and incredible joy.

He slumped onto her, nestling his head against her shoulder.

So sated that she couldn't move, Sabrina didn't mind the weight of his body one little bit. She relished it. Her eyes fluttered closed and her lips curved in a smile.

The feeling of his flesh against her only added to the drowsy contentment. He rolled to one side, but still she could feel the length of his body against hers, floating away in a dreamy lethargy as his hands moved gently over her, still caressing.

After a while he picked her up in his arms. She knew she should leave, but she couldn't even rouse herself enough to open her eyes. He laid her down on cool sheets and stretched out beside her, pulling her possessively close as his arms tightened around her. She nestled into the crook of his shoulder, enveloped in the smell of his skin, feeling his flesh against her lips. This was contentment. This was where she wanted to be.

SHE OPENED HER EYES to see the sky pale in the first light of dawn. Turning her head on the pillow, she saw Michael beside her. He lay on his back, his face relaxed in sleep, vulnerable and heartbreaking and wonderful.

She resisted the urge to touch him, to kiss his lips. Carefully, so as not to wake him, she slipped out of bed. She had to get away from here.

Last night had been wonderful and absolute madness at the same time. It should never have happened. Yet she couldn't regret it for a second.

But now it was morning. And last night didn't change anything—it only made things more complicated. She would have to face him eventually, but not now, not yet.

Heading for the sitting room, she began picking up her clothes, then turned for one last look. He lay on his back, the white sheet against his golden skin, and for a moment she was tempted to crawl back in beside him.

But then she turned resolutely, dressed and left.

The cool morning breeze ruffled her hair as she stepped out of the house, but it wasn't cold enough to make her feel chilled to the bone this way. She wrapped her arms tightly around her body, hugging herself against the coldness inside.

She loved him, as she'd never loved anybody before. As she could never imagine loving anybody again. But it wouldn't work for them.

Pausing at the gates, she looked back at the house, standing silent and still in the early-morning light. This was a world where she didn't belong.

It took an hour and a half to walk home through the waking city. Time she desperately needed in order to think. Her head whirled with a dizzying jumble of needs and desires. Why couldn't she just let it happen?

The walk did nothing to clear her head at all, or raise her spirits. By the time she turned onto her own street, she felt overwhelmed by the longing for what could not be.

She had almost reached her house when Michael got out of the Jag parked in front.

Tight-lipped and pale with anger, he stepped onto the sidewalk to block her way. "Where have you been?"

Numb with shock, she stopped. "I walked home. What are you doing here?"

"Didn't you think I would come?"

"No, I didn't."

"You're kidding me." His brow furrowed in pained disbelief. "You didn't think...after what we had together last night..."

"Please let's not talk about last night."

He went still and his voice took on an ominous note. "Why shouldn't we talk about last night?"

She turned away and his hand closed around her arm, none-too-gently, and turned her to face him. "Why shouldn't we talk about last night?" he repeated.

"There's nothing to talk about." Couldn't he see her heart was breaking and she just wanted to be left alone? She pulled away and walked quickly up the path.

He was right behind her, holding the screen door open while she fumbled for her key. His tension made her clumsy as she fitted it into the lock. She felt weary and heartsick, and the last thing she wanted was to fight.

"Please, Michael, I'm very tired right now. If we have to talk, can't it be later?"

"No."

She stepped over the threshold and he followed her in.

"My God, Sabrina! I wake up and you're gone. Not even a note. I come here and you're not home. What was I supposed to think?"

"I think you're making too much of this." Half-turned away, she put a hand to her brow and closed her aching eyes. "As you can see, I'm perfectly safe. And now I really wish you'd leave."

"What happened?" He cupped the nape of her neck, moving around to face her, gently but forcefully holding her captive. "Last night . . ."

"Last night was a terrible mistake. . . ."

"How can you say that?" He brought her face closer to his as his hot gaze descended to her lips. "Sabrina . . ."

"No, Michael." She tore away from him, trembling in response to the tormented sound of his voice. "Nothing has changed. All those reasons we had before for not getting involved. They still exist. We've made a mistake, Michael. I think we'd better forget about it before somebody gets hurt," she finished, low and anguished.

"This is crazy." He turned away for a moment and ran a hand through his hair. "Well, I can't forget." He spun around to face her, anger and hurt warring on his face.

"What can I say? There's no way this can work."

For a long moment he only looked at her, with bleak, empty eyes. "So where do we go from here, Sabrina? And please don't tell me I have to forget about it."

"I don't know, I don't know," she groaned and sank her head in her hands. "We've got to be sensible. You know this won't work."

He reached out and laced a hand through the short hair at the nape of her neck, forcing her to look up at him. "How do you know it won't work unless we give it a chance?"

It was so hard to resist the entreaty in his eyes. "It's all too complicated." She felt utterly miserable.

"It doesn't have to be." His thumb traced the line of her mouth, a drugging caress. It was so hard to fight the need, yet she struggled to do what she had to do.

"It isn't that easy. You're a Worth."

He gave a small smile. "Guilty as charged. But does that mean we can't give ourselves a chance? See what happens?"

"And if it doesn't work, what then?"

"You want guarantees?"

"Yes," she whispered, hearing the finality in her own voice.

He expelled his breath in a long sigh. "We could be dead tomorrow. There are no guarantees."

"We both know there are too many reasons why this *cannot* happen."

"But I want you, and you want me."

"And what if I said I *don't* want you."

"I'd say you were lying."

Before she knew what was happening, he pulled her into his arms and took her mouth in a hard, possessive kiss. She struggled to pull away but he held her tightly. With a little moan of defeat, she sagged against him. All she could do was resist the urge to hold him, the urge to kiss him back, until finally he let her go.

Breathing rapidly, voice ragged with emotion, he looked down into her eyes. "I still say you're lying." He turned and walked out, closing the door quietly behind him.

She stood frozen to the spot until she heard the car slowly pull away, and then the tears began coursing down her cheeks.

He was hurt, he was lonely. She was the only person he could talk to about Colin and he was reaching out to her for consolation, for physical closeness. Even a strong man like Michael needed a shoulder to lean on. Right now he needed *her.* But when that need no longer existed, what then?

8

SABRINA STEPPED OFF the packed streetcar to the familiar roar of traffic and the sound of honking horns. The noise was preferable to the press of bodies in the crowded trolley. Right now, however, she could barely cope with either. And yet here she was, heading back into the pressure cooker.

She needed to be somewhere quiet and serene where she could collect her thoughts, calm her soul. But somehow, she'd get through this day and work, just as she had all the other days since that Saturday morning two weeks ago when Michael had walked out of her house. As always, her thoughts obsessively returned to Michael, and to the glorious night they'd had together. There was undeniably something wonderful between them, and no reason why they couldn't be happy...for a while. But it wouldn't work, she told herself for the thousandth time.

Up ahead, people were clustered in front of the main entrance to Worth's. Strange, she thought. No big sales were scheduled until the end of the month. But it didn't register completely. Nothing really registered these days.

The crowd was so large, it blocked the pavement, forcing pedestrians out onto the road and disrupting traffic. Cars were honking, drivers were swearing, bicycle couriers were nimbly dodging around everybody.

As she got closer, she saw people marching with placards. To her horror several were blazoned with the slogan, BAH HUMBUG, EBENEZER WORTH!

"Oh my God!" It couldn't be.

Quickening her pace, she reached the edge of the crowd. "What's happening? What are you people—Charlie!" she exclaimed at the sight of a familiar white head. He turned at the sound of her voice and made his way through the crowd toward her.

"I'm so sorry. I'm trying to get these people to go home."

"Who are they?"

She looked around in dismay. Most of the protesters seemed to be elderly. She recognized some of the volunteer marshals who belonged to the same seniors' club as Charlie, but young mothers were there, too, pushing children in strollers, or toting babies in carriers strapped to their chests. On the fringes she even noticed a couple of derelicts, clutching brown paper bags and watching the action.

"When I was down at the seniors' club I mentioned about the parade in passing, but I never meant for this to happen. I never knew anything about it until this morning. I got a call from George asking me to spearhead the protest," he said in disgust. "He wanted me to come down in my Santa suit, for heaven's sake."

She groaned. "What a mess! Charlie, we have to do something. Oh my God, there's Mr. Stevenson."

Through the glass door at the top of the steps she could see his round face, jowls quivering with outrage. His yes-men stood by, all frowning their disapproval at the gathering below. She felt thankful for one small mercy: at least Michael was out of town and wouldn't see all this. Especially since most of the slogans were mocking him personally.

She caught sight of another placard and winced.

MICHAEL WORTHLESS, HANDS OFF OUR PARADE!

A siren wailed, and within minutes half a dozen policemen were moving through the crowd, getting people off the road and back onto the pavement.

"Okay, folks, break it up." The biggest and burliest of the officers patiently helped a mother get her stroller out of the way, then turned to the elderly woman standing beside Sabrina. With her picture hat, flowered dress and a white purse over one arm she was a dead ringer for the Queen Mother, except for the placard she carried over one shoulder saying DOWN WITH THE FASCIST SANTA KILLER!

The policeman spoke to her, not unkindly. "Let's all move along now."

"Forget it, you Nazi!" The Queen Mother whirled around and grabbed Sabrina's wrist. "We'll form a human chain. They'll have to drag us out of here!"

Which the police promptly did.

AN HOUR LATER she was sitting in the local police station, along with all the other protesters. An officer had come in and told them they would be released when a friend or relative signed them out. When her turn came, she'd called Anya, assuming she even had a job to return to, after the nightmarish scene that followed the protest.

After trying to get the crowd to break up, the police began leading people, some kicking and protesting, to the paddy wagons.

She'd felt sorry for the huge cop who had to escort a tiny white-haired lady. What could he do with an elderly woman who was beating at him with her placard? She had been warbling, "When I was your age, young man, I chained myself to the doors of City Hall to get women the vote!"

"Yeah, yeah. Sure, grandma. Mind your head there." He settled her into the paddy wagon.

He had come back and taken Sabrina by the arm. Beneath the peaked cap his face glowed red and his forehead was beaded with sweat. "You, too. Come along now."

"No, you don't understand. I'm the coordinator…."

"Then you should be ashamed of yourself, getting all these old people involved in this mess."

She winced at the memory and sank farther down into her seat. Walter Stevenson was probably chortling with satisfaction right now. Here was his chance to tear up her employment contract.

Over in one corner the Queen Mother was loudly berating every authority figure from the prime minister on down as a bunch of fascists, while the little old white-haired suffragette sat on a couch nearby, bemoaning her fate in this "hellhole."

Sabrina suppressed a smile as she looked around the pleasant room. It seemed to be some kind of lounge with comfortable furniture and prints on the wall, and even a pop machine in one corner.

The man next to her on the couch patted the old lady's hand. "Don't worry, Martha. John is coming down from the home. He'll get us all out."

Sabrina turned to Charlie and felt dismayed to see him sitting hunched and dejected in his chair.

"This is all my fault. The blame rests squarely on my shoulders."

"That's not true, Charlie."

"If I hadn't opened my big mouth…"

"How were you supposed to know George would get so carried away?"

He shook his head. Even his smart mustache seemed to be drooping a little. "I should have just kept my big mouth shut."

"If it comes to that, so should I."

"Here comes one of the screws," muttered the old lady in the corner, the light of battle in her eyes again.

Charlie's gaze shifted over Sabrina's shoulder. "I think you're about to be sprung from this hellhole, Sabrina."

She turned to see Michael standing in the doorway. For a moment, as she met his gaze, nothing else existed. These past two weeks had felt like years. She'd missed him so much. This was what it meant to love someone. That just the sight of him could give her so much joy.

"Sabrina." He moved toward her.

She had to say something, do something. She turned to Charlie, but before she could introduce them, the older man held out his hand.

"Mr. Worth, I'm Charlie Andersen. And before you say anything, I want you to know this whole mess was my fault. Sabrina had nothing to do with it. Whatever you were going to say to her, say it to me."

Michael shook the offered hand. His face was grave, but there was a hint of laughter in his eyes as he shrugged. "Well, okay... darling, are you all right?"

Sabrina choked on a giggle. Charlie stared at Michael for a moment as if he'd gone mad, then his eyes twinkled and a grin broke across his distinguished old face.

"This young man of yours is all right, Sabrina."

She blushed and Michael gave her a keen look, then smiled. "There was no harm done. Things like this happen all the time... to Sabrina."

She groaned and rolled her eyes. "You can say that again."

Charlie patted her arm. "Mr. Worth, you've got a wonderful girl here."

"Yes, I know." The warmth in Michael's eyes took her breath away.

"Mr. Worth? You're Mr. Worth?" The tiny old lady raised herself from the couch and stepped closer to wag a bony finger in his face. "Now listen here, young man. I was speaking to your mother last night and she said you always were a wild one."

Michael reared back from the accusing finger and shot Sabrina a bemused look.

"Now, now, Martha, let's not keep Mr. Worth. He's a busy man with things to do." Charlie gently took her arm and led her back to her seat, casting them an apologetic look over his shoulder.

"You're all a bunch of fascists!" came an angry grumble from the other old lady in the corner.

Sabrina felt the corners of her mouth beginning to twitch and noticed that Michael, after his initial bemusement, was also fighting back a grin. He looked down at her, his eyes glowing with an intoxicating mixture of devilment and appreciation.

"We'd better get going. Can I give you a lift, Mr. Andersen?"

"Call me Charlie. And thanks all the same, but I'm expecting my daughter any minute."

With a wave to Charlie, Sabrina walked quickly out of the building, with Michael right behind. Reaching the gleaming green Jag in the parking lot, she collapsed against it as they both exploded in laughter.

"You should have seen the look on your face!" she gasped, finally able to get out the words.

"Where do you find them?" he choked out.

"Come on, they're not that bad." Drawing a deep breath, she began to calm down.

"And not that sane, either."

She shook her head. "Dear old Mrs. Entwistle. She's nearly ninety and really quite sweet."

"You mean, really quite batty. But you're right, she is rather sweet. And so are you. Do me a favor and never change, Sabrina. Even when you're ninety."

Suddenly her throat tightened and it was hard to breathe. Standing in the middle of the drab parking lot, everything else receded except the need that pulled them together.

"I think we'd better get going. I have a lot of work to do." She turned away and fumbled with the door handle.

His hand closed over hers, warm and firm. "I'd rather go someplace and talk."

She quickly removed her fingers and put her hands behind her back. "I don't think that would be a good idea, Michael."

He gave her a long unreadable look, then opened the door for her. As she got into the passenger seat, she darted him a quick glance and met an implacable, steady gaze that sent a tremor racing through her. He wasn't going to give up. But that wasn't what scared her. What scared her was knowing she wouldn't be able to keep him at a distance for long.

He got in and started the engine, then drove out of the lot while she stared hard out the window. She couldn't look at him, couldn't cope with her emotions.

She turned to him. She had to find something to say to fill up the silence. "How was London?"

"Long and tedious without you there."

"Please, Michael, don't..."

He let out his breath in a sigh of frustration, gripping the wheel so tightly that his knuckles were white. The tension was becoming unbearable.

She turned her face back to the window. She was so in love with him, and he was such a wonderful man, but he could be the most heartbreaking thing that ever happened to her.

After a while she came out of her dark musings and realized they were heading away from downtown, away from the store. She turned to him quickly, feeling a little panicked. "Where are you going?"

He gave her a quick glance, then looked back at the road. His lips curved in a slow smile. "I'm kidnapping you," he said in a husky drawl.

"What!" She jerked upright and grabbed at the dash for support. She couldn't afford to be alone with him.

He glanced over at her again and she caught her breath. His face was lit with a boyish, mischievous light. She had to fight the urge to reach over and brush back the rakish lock of dark hair that curled down onto his forehead. My God, how could she keep up her resistance when everything about him affected her so strongly?

"It's been the longest two weeks of my life since I last saw you and I finally have you to myself. I just want to spend some time alone with you."

His words sent a thrill of pure pleasure racing through her, and pure pain. She wanted to be with him, too, but she couldn't trust herself. She couldn't let this happen.

"Michael, I have work to do. I can't take off just like that. I have a meeting with Jonathan."

The low gray clouds were clearing as they drove east along Lakeshore Boulevard, past the industrial jumble of wharf buildings and loading machinery serving the lake freighters.

He picked up the car phone between them. "Call him. Reschedule."

"I can't. This is important. I can't let my personal life interfere with my job."

He let the phone drop back into its cradle with a clatter and sent her a quick mocking glance. "Don't you mean, you shouldn't let your job interfere with your personal life?"

She sighed and looked out the window without seeing any of the scenery. "We can't ignore the fact that we work together."

He expelled a heavy breath. "Look, Sabrina. I know we decided that mixing business with pleasure was bad news—" the tired resignation sharpened, becoming adamant and passionate "—but what's happening between us is impossible to ignore."

"I'm not trying to ignore it. On the contrary, I'm fighting it very hard. It's bad for us. We can't give in to it."

"Sabrina—"

"Michael." She turned and cut him off. "Can't we just spend some time together without letting all this get in the way?"

"Can you?"

His quiet voice disturbed her and she turned back to look out of the window. On the right was the beginning of lakefront parkland. In the distance she could see the tall brick houses of Woodbine Avenue, only a few blocks from her place. Was he planning on going there?

But as they passed an inlet filled with small craft gently bobbing on the waves, he suddenly slowed and turned off the boulevard into Ashbridges Bay Park.

In the midmorning quiet, the parking lot was almost deserted. He pulled into a spot close to the beach, shaded by an avenue of maples in their brilliant autumn colors. He shut off the ignition and turned in his seat to look at her squarely.

"Can't we be just friends, Michael?"

"That wouldn't be enough for me. I can't ignore the way you make me feel."

Not the way he felt about her. The way she *made* him feel. He was talking about desire and she was talking about love. "Well, you have to."

She threw open the door and jumped out of the car, striding across the parking lot toward the water with tense steps. Torn and confused, she couldn't risk being so close to him, couldn't risk losing control.

Crossing the boardwalk, she stepped onto the sand, heading without thinking for the jumble of limestone boulders crowning the shallow sweep of the bay. She had to get away, put some space between them, or she was lost.

Her feet sank into the warm sand, the breeze off the lake played through her hair and felt like velvet on her bare arms. It was a spectacular day. Spread out before her, the vast expanse of water was a patchwork of muted grays and sparkling turquoise. In the distance, boat sails gleamed in the bright sunlight, while gulls wheeled and screeched overhead.

Michael caught up with her, his warm fingers lacing through hers, pulling her to a stop. She snatched her hand away from the touch that burned through her like fire. Standing on a boulder above him, she looked down into eyes filled with loneliness.

"Please, don't run away. I agree to any terms you want. If you want to keep it just friends, I'll try, I promise." He squinted away across the water for a moment, then brought his tormented gaze back to her. "Just stay with me, talk to me."

All her resistance was seeping away and it frightened her. But what harm was there in just talking? And what else could they do in such a public place?

"What do you want to talk about?"

"You choose. Anything you want. I just want to be where you are." He let out a sigh and closed his eyes for a moment.

"The parade."

He opened them and looked at her with a tinge of exasperation. "We'll discuss that later. I don't want to talk about work. Pick something else."

"Tell me about your wife, then."

Fleeting surprise crossed his face, then he squinted off into the distance. "I don't want to talk about Lorraine, either," he said impatiently, then looked back up at her. "Anything else, not Lorraine."

"But I want to know about the woman you married."

He held her gaze for a long moment, then moved over to the boulders at the water's edge and sat down, uncaring of the knife-edge crease in his charcoal-gray wool suit.

After a moment of hesitation, she lowered herself beside him, careful not to sit too close. Desire filled the air between them.

"What do you want to know?"

She turned to meet his eyes filled with an intimacy and warmth that made her feel cherished. It would be madness to allow herself to bask in the feeling.

"Everything."

His brow furrowed as he looked out across the lake. He said nothing for a long moment and she thought he wasn't going to comply.

"We met when I was at Oxford. I was eighteen. She was twenty-five and worked in the local pub. Lorraine was quite a . . . sexual creature. All the guys were crazy about her."

"And, of course, you were crazy about her, too," she said with a lightness she didn't feel. It hurt to even think about him with another woman, but she'd been the one who had brought up the subject.

He shrugged. "I'd never had any girlfriends before. I was old before my time, in many ways, but when it came to women...I was...um...uninitiated...."

Like father, like son, she mused silently.

"I was flabbergasted that she singled me out," Michael continued.

Was it any wonder? She traced his chiseled profile, his crisply curling black hair. At eighteen he must have been a young Adonis.

"And of course, I fell madly in love." He was far away, lost in memories that clearly gave him no pleasure. "With all those other guys after her, I couldn't believe my luck when she told me she loved me, too."

The hurt in his voice sent a stab of pain through her. After all these years, was he still in love with Lorraine?

"Anyway, before I knew it, there was a baby on the way. She had quit her job at the pub, we got married and she moved in with me." He shifted restlessly and tossed a couple of pebbles into the water. When he spoke again, his voice was cold. "When I told my mother, she had a fit. She told me not to be such a fool. That Lorraine was only interested in me for my money." He stopped with a contemptuous twist of his mouth.

Automatically, Sabrina reached out and put a hand on his arm to comfort him.

"She offered Lorraine a settlement if she'd have an abortion and agree to an annulment. Lorraine refused. I saw it as a sign that she really loved me." He gave a short humorless laugh. "Boy, was I wrong."

"What happened?"

"Sybil cut off my allowance. I didn't care. I was quite prepared to quit school and go to work, but fortunately I landed a good part-time job that enabled me to keep a roof over our heads. I thought I was doing quite well." Now he shot her a twisted smile. "But Sybil was right. It wasn't what Lorraine had bargained for. She'd expected to be living in the lap of luxury. We began to fight."

Until now she'd had no reason to think the marriage had been anything but idyllic. Hearing the awful truth made her feel even more pained for him.

"After Colin was born, I think she expected Sybil to relent and reinstate my allowance, but when I told her that I didn't want to take any more money from my mother, that we would have to live on what I earned, she was brutally honest about the way she really felt about me."

"Oh, Michael..." She could imagine only too clearly everything he left unsaid.

He shrugged away her compassion. "It was a lesson worth learning."

Now she could finally understand why he overreacted so much to the situation between her and Colin. It must have seemed like history repeating itself.

"And then she left, leaving the baby with me. Five days later I heard she was dead in a skiing accident. She'd been with another man. But my love had died before she did."

Sabrina stared silently out at the water. The lake and sky dissolved into a blue-gray blur as tears filled her eyes. She loved him. God, how she loved him.

"Now that I've told you everything there is to say about Lorraine—" his voice softened, became husky "—I want to talk about us. I dreamed about you last night, about making love to you." His fingers trailed slowly up her arm, sending violent tremors racing through her. "I want to hold you...."

"No!" she choked out. "You promised."

"I know, but I need to hold you, to be with you. I need you."

"But for how long?" She couldn't suppress the questions that tormented her. "How long will it take you to realize that we have nothing in common? That we come from two different worlds and that I'm all wrong for you, Michael?"

"What are you talking about, two different worlds?"

"You've grown up with power and privilege and money. You can go anywhere you want, do anything you want, have anything you want. Your family has built this incredible business empire, with stores around the globe. My parents run a modest little cottage resort. They're just plain hardworking folks."

"Then I don't see how we're any different. *I'm* just a plain hardworking person—"

"You're Michael Worth!" she cut in. Was she not being clear enough? Why couldn't he see for himself that chasm between them? "Your world and my world are separate. It's not so easy to cross that border."

He looked at her for a moment, then gave a low, ironic laugh. "Life can be so damned unfair. You just told me that being Michael Worth means having it all. But right now what I want is out of reach, because of who I am." He stopped in frustration, his voice suddenly low and weary. "I just want to be with you."

His anguished need was her undoing. He lowered his head to hers. Her lips merged with his instinctively. When he crushed her to him, she felt a wild torrent of desire.

He pulled away a fraction. "I want to make love to you here, between the water and the sky." He needed her close, so close, he wanted to absorb her into himself. "It's been hell trying to keep my mind on business these past two weeks. Don't you know, Sabrina, that you fill my thoughts day and night? This hunger for you is tearing me apart."

"That's crazy," she said in a whisper. But the responsive arching of her body belied her words. Her every movement made him shudder and burn.

"I know." He couldn't stop himself from taking her mouth again.

Then he pulled away, gulping air into his lungs like a drowning man. When he spoke, his voice didn't even sound like his own. "You know what's even crazier? I have no defenses against you. You make me laugh, you make me cry. God knows you've brought me trembling to my knees with a deeper need than I've ever known before."

From behind, came the sound of children's voices calling and laughing, and she drew away from him abruptly, but he held on to her hand and squeezed it tight.

"I missed you."

Just the low, husky sound of his voice made her tremble. She stared out at the gray horizon.

"Did you miss me, too?"

She wanted to deny it, but he cupped her chin and turned her face toward his, forcing her to look up at him. The piercing intensity in his eyes made her feel suddenly very shy.

Nodding her head, she could only whisper, "Yes."

He heaved a deep breath and expelled it in what sounded like relief. "I wanted to call. But I thought maybe if you had some time and space to think about us . . ."

She turned her head away, and drew her hand from his. Picking up a pebble lying at her feet, she tossed it into the water three feet below, watching as the ripples spread out and died away. "You're right. I do need time to think."

"What's there to think about, Sabrina?"

At the tension in his voice, she darted him a glance and saw the frustrated look of a man who was sick to death of going over the same old argument. And yet she couldn't give up. He was who he was, and nothing could change that.

Even if by some miracle he could love her back, they didn't live in a vacuum. How could she ever be truly accepted into his world? As Sybil had correctly assumed about Lorraine, there would be many quick to conclude that she'd pursued him because of his wealth.

"Don't you understand? If this thing between us was meant to happen, it would feel right. I wouldn't have any reservations." He made an impatient sound, but she pressed on. "You come from a different world...."

He groaned with frustration. "Yes, I know—so you keep saying—but what the hell does that have to do with us?"

"Everything."

He swore angrily and stood up, shoving his hands into his pockets. She rose to her feet as he stared out over the ruffled waves with a bleak expression on his face.

"No. You're talking about two separate realities. I'm talking about making a world of our own."

"That won't work." The truth of her words weighed on her heart like a millstone. "My life has been so limited, but you grew up knowing that anything was possible, *because you're a Worth*. It shaped your attitudes and your view of the world, just as my upbringing shaped me."

He turned slowly toward her, incredulous. "You're a snob!"

She shook her head. "I just don't think it would be a good idea for us to start anything."

"It's too late. We've already started something."

"Then we have to stop." She turned and began walking away.

His footsteps rang on the rocks behind her, then she felt his hand on her arm, spinning her around. She almost lost her balance and had to grab on to his forearms, but he held on to her tightly.

"So what you're really saying is, you have no faith in me. You don't want to give us a chance." His eyes filled with anger and pain.

"That's not true," she said thickly as tears began blurring her vision. "You're just twisting things around. You're confusing me."

"How? How am I twisting things around? For God's sake, Sabrina, I want you. I think we could be really good together. What are you afraid of?"

I'm afraid that you don't love me the way I love you. But she couldn't admit that fear.

"I'm afraid that we could get in too deep and one of us, if not both, will end up getting hurt."

"But, darling, that's the chance everybody takes...."

She shook her head. "No, Michael. It could mess up my job. It could mess up my life. Can't we just be friends?"

"Could you really be satisfied with just that?"

No, no she couldn't, but she said, "I have to be."

She pulled away and stepped down onto the sand, then began walking back toward the parking lot. When she reached the car she turned to see him still standing where she'd left him, staring out at the lake. After a moment he turned and began slowly trudging across the beach.

When he reached the car he paused for a moment, fixing her with a long, unreadable look. She couldn't say anything, couldn't even tear her gaze away. Finally he unlocked her door before going around to the driver's side.

He was suddenly so closed, so aloof. Once more the remote man she had first met in his office. Her heart contracted with despair. If she was doing the right thing, why did she feel so utterly miserable?

9

UNDER A BRILLIANT blue sky, the small boat sped across the open lake toward the island that the Worths had owned since the turn of the century. Sabrina leaned forward slightly and strained to hear as the weather-beaten marina operator yelled above the noise of the outboard motor.

"You got all your groceries in there already. The missus stocked the fridge and made up the beds like Mr. Colin asked."

"That's great. Thank you," she yelled back.

She must be crazy. After that final conversation with Michael, what was she doing going to his family cottage? He had returned to London the very next day, even though she'd heard from Anya that the problems over there didn't require his personal attention this time. But he had obviously decided to give up on her and give them both more space to let things get back to normal. She should have been glad about that, but she was miserable with missing him.

At least some things were working out, though. Anya and Perry were engaged to be married. Which only reaffirmed her philosophy of relationships. If it was meant to happen, nothing, not even distance, was an obstacle. The only question that remained was, would Michael transfer Anya to London, or Perry to Toronto? The last thing she wanted to dwell on was her own hopeless situation with Michael. But it was no big surprise—she'd known it from the very beginning.

Better to dwell on what *was* working out for her. Through Jonathan, who was in touch with Michael in London, she'd convinced Michael to keep the parade going if she could find other sponsors to cover half the cost. Fortunately it had been easy finding several other companies eager to associate themselves with a good cause, and reap excellent publicity in the bargain.

As for Colin, he had begun his first year at the University of Toronto and, although he was only working Saturdays now, Michael had promoted him to salesclerk in Menswear.

Ever since then, Colin had seemed more like his old self. The schoolboy crush was over. He had made friends with some of his fellow workers and students, ensuring a healthy social life that left him too busy to chase her.

There was some comfort in finally seeing Colin back on the right track, so when he offered her the use of the Worth cottage in the Muskoka Lakes for a long weekend, she had jumped at the chance.

Anya, her usual source of well-informed gossip, had told her that Michael had ordered the refurbishing of the summer home, not far from where Sabrina grew up in the rugged beauty of Northern Ontario.

Foolish as it was, she wanted to see the place where Michael had spent his childhood summers. What sort of little boy had he been? Mischievous and willful like his son, before manhood claimed him with its terrible weight of tragedy and responsibility? Or had he always been the loner who sought solitude in remote places, like the mountains of Nepal, places as remote as his own soul?

She knew she shouldn't be coming here, she shouldn't allow herself to care, but she was tired of being sensible.

She'd already done the smart thing by pushing him away. Now this was for herself. She couldn't have Michael, but she couldn't stop loving him, either.

And it was a glorious day, still unbelievably warm in the lingering Indian summer. The woods crowding the shore were aflame in all their autumn glory.

With the parade only a week away on the first weekend in November, all the arrangements were in place and now it was the calm before the storm. She needed this time to herself, and she wasn't going to feel guilty about that, either.

Up ahead, the island was swiftly growing larger. Like a giant egg of glacier-smoothed granite, it rose steeply out of the water on one side, then sloped gently down for a good half mile to meet the waves again.

She caught a glimpse of black rooftop at the highest point, but otherwise there was nothing to be seen except the dark green cloak of spruce and jack pine, splashed here and there with golden birches.

The motor slowed to an idle hum as the boat approached the heavy pilings of a cedar dock, set next to a large boathouse. The caretaker grabbed a mooring ring and hung on while Sabrina tossed her duffel bag onto the dock and scrambled out.

"Okay, then, miss, I'll be seeing you Sunday evening. Have a nice weekend."

She waved and watched him putting away, then turned to climb the steps leading up from the boathouse. Farther along the shore lay a crescent of sandy beach and up above, through the dark pines, peeked a fieldstone chimney and the maple-stained wood siding of a huge home with a screened porch all along the front.

She let out a low whistle. Nice cottage, but she hadn't expected anything less from the Worths.

Unlocking the front door, she stepped into a large, well-proportioned living room. She'd expected the house to be a little musty from years of sitting virtually deserted, but instead it smelled of furniture polish and the fresh, pine-scented breeze wafting in through the open window.

The brilliant sunshine gleamed on pine antiques and splashed over braided rugs and English chintz upholstery. Despite the impression of affluence, the room had a cosy colonial charm that pleased her. She could relax here.

Upstairs, there were four large bedrooms to choose from. She felt positively spoiled as she settled on the big front room looking out over the expanse of lake dotted with little islands in the distance.

As she threw her bag on the bed, a loud banging from below startled her. She hadn't heard the boat coming back, but obviously the caretaker had forgotten something.

Racing lightly down the stairs, she flung open the door to see Colin's grinning face.

"Hi. Can Sabrina come out to play?"

Words failed her for a moment and she could only gape at him. "What are *you* doing here?"

He shouldered past her through the doorway. "I got to thinking a vacation would be fun. What's the matter? You don't look too pleased to see me."

His cocky grin nettled her into speech.

"I'm not. As I said, what are you doing here?"

"C'mon, Sabrina. Don't be like that. We could have a lot of fun together."

The charming boyish smile was wasted on her. She gritted her teeth. "How did you get here?"

"My boat." He jerked a thumb back toward the dock.

"Fine." She turned away toward the stairs. "Then you go get it started, because you're taking me back."

He laughed behind her. "But, Sabrina . . ."

Whirling around, she strode back to poke a finger in his chest. "Don't Sabrina me. You had all this planned, didn't you?"

"Well, not to begin with." He stumbled back, slightly alarmed, but the grin stayed on his face.

In disgust she headed for the stairs again.

"Hey, where are you going?"

"To get my things."

She snatched her bag, angry with Colin, but even more furious with herself. All this time she'd managed to convince herself he'd got over his infatuation. Like a blind fool, she'd been so caught up in her problems with Michael, she hadn't paid much attention to Colin.

Dragging her bag downstairs to an empty hall, she headed down to the dock, finding Colin stretched out on a lounge chair. Behind his dark glasses, she knew he was watching her approach.

"You know, Sabrina, you're being much too melodramatic about this. What's the harm? So we stay here and have a nice weekend together."

"Are you going to drive me back or not?"

"No, I'm not."

"Very well." She stepped over to look down at the boat and her heart sank. It wasn't just a little outboard. It was a sleek racing vessel, the skittish kind that could flip over spectacularly with the wrong handling. So what? She grew up around boats. She'd drive herself back.

"Sabrina?"

Turning, she saw Colin grin as he dangled a key chain on his fingertip, then made a show of dropping it into the pocket of his loose madras shirt. "You might need these."

This was absolutely the last straw. She dropped her bag and sank to her knees on the dock, tired, fed up and perfectly willing to toss Colin Worth to the catfish, lounge chair and all.

"It's a long drive back to Toronto in the same day."

Refusing to respond, she fixed her gaze on the opposite shore.

"I tell you what. I'll drive you back tomorrow." His soft voice cajoled her. "It's so nice here. Why don't we just enjoy it?"

She was too tired to argue anymore. She got to her feet and pointed a threatening finger at him. "Fine. But you'd better not try any nonsense with me. Got that?"

"What do you take me for? You're too old for me, remember?"

The incorrigible smile that broke out across his face brought an unwilling quirk to her own lips. After all, this was Colin. He was acting more like a mischievous kid than an adolescent with seduction on his mind. She had nothing to fear from him. Besides, she could handle him. She bent to pick up her bag, but he had already jumped to his feet.

"Let me."

He whisked the bag from her hands, then dropped it on the dock again so that he could put a hand on her shoulder and send her toppling into the lounge chair. Before she could utter a squeak of protest he had grabbed her ankles and swung her legs up onto the padded cushion.

"Now relax. That's what you're up here for, remember?"

As he took her case up to the house, she leaned back and let out a huge sigh. Just one day. What could it hurt? She took a deep breath of the pine-scented air, luxuriating in the warmth of the sun on her face, feeling it soak through her jeans and caress her arms, bared by the T-shirt.

It was so quiet. It really was glorious to be out of the city, in this peaceful environment that she missed more than she liked to admit.

What if it had been Michael who was here with her? She closed her eyes on a tiny sigh. Would she be able to keep up her resistance under these circumstances? She wouldn't have a prayer.

Just the thought of having a whole weekend alone together set off a shudder deep inside her. Caressed by the warm breeze, she felt deliciously languid. How easy it would be to allow herself to forget about the outside world. How idyllic to be able to spend the days getting to know each other, the nights making love. This could be their own little paradise, if they were any other two people in the world.

Something bumped against the dock and she opened her eyes to see Michael stepping out of the caretaker's boat, followed by Anya. For a moment she could only stare in disbelief.

She must have fallen asleep. She must be dreaming. He was supposed to be five thousand miles away, not standing here in a well-worn pair of jeans and a red plaid shirt, helping Anya out of the boat after him. Sabrina jerked upright in the lounge chair and stumbled to her feet. It was impossible, but he was here.

"What the hell . . ."

She turned at the sound of Colin's exclamation to see him standing behind her with his mouth hanging open, holding a tray with two glasses of lemonade.

Michael could barely restrain the urge to burst out laughing at the ludicrous expression on his son's face. With an effort he kept this voice casual and scooped up one of the frosty glasses.

"Why, Colin, how very thoughtful of you." He drank off the lemonade in one long grateful swallow.

An overnight transatlantic flight followed almost immediately by a three-hour drive had left him in need of some reviving. He set the glass back down on the tray.

"What the hell are you doing here?" Colin finally found his voice and gave him a furious glare.

"I had a ton of work to do, but I decided I needed a rest. I brought Anya along so we could both have a little working holiday."

Without another word, Colin turned and ran heavily back up the steps.

Anya frowned in concern as she watched the boy go, then turned to Sabrina with a speaking look that made him smile. He'd have to make sure they had the opportunity for some private girl talk, because Anya wouldn't be satisfied until she had every gory detail. Then she turned to him. "I'm going to go change into something cooler."

In her twill trousers and heavy sweater, Anya's cheeks were pink and her forehead already beaded with sweat in the afternoon sun. Carrying her small case, she followed Colin on up to the house.

Finally he could turn his attention to Sabrina. His exhaustion vanished in an instant.

After those endless, unbearable three weeks apart, all he wanted was to take her into his arms and kiss her, carry her on up to the house and make love to her, slowly and sweetly until the ache of missing her was assuaged. If there were some way to get rid of Colin and Anya, he'd do it, and to hell with the consequences.

"How did you know we were here?" She sounded breathless and her eyes widened in desperation as if she wanted to escape. A shocking sense of hurt tore through him.

"Anya told me where you were. My housekeeper told me Colin had gone away for the weekend. I put two and two together and took a chance you'd both be here—"

"It's not what you think," she cut in anxiously.

He stepped closer, needing to be near her. "What I think is that my son is madly infatuated with you and I can't blame him because so am I," he finished in a murmur, as he looked down into her startled eyes.

Her lips were so close, so tempting. He need only bend his head a little.... Just the memory of that lush mouth softly yielding against his own, those lips parting in urgent response, made every muscle in his body tighten with desire.

The hunger must have been betrayed in his face. She swiftly braced one hand on his chest and he could feel her trembling. "Please, Michael."

After a second's hesitation, he sighed and stepped back. She let out a long, unsteady breath.

"How've you been?" he asked.

She could hear the iron control tightening his voice and said hurriedly, "Really busy. The parade's heating up. It'll be crazy when I get back." After blurting out the nervous, stilted words, she had to turn away.

He reached out and put a hand under her chin, slowly turning her face toward him. His expression was gentle, his mouth curved in a small smile. "I don't care about the work. I meant, how have *you* been?"

"Fine." *Missing you.* But to admit it to him would be madness. "So what do you plan on doing, Michael?"

His smile widened, carefree and boyish, and her heart flipped over. "Why, have a holiday, of course. I think we all deserve a break, don't you?"

She stepped away from him and shook her head. "I was planning on going back tomorrow."

"There's no need now. I even brought Anya up here."

He seemed to understand everything—all her doubts and fears. "Well..." She hesitated, tempted just to be with him, crazy and dangerous as that might be, when the slightest look, the merest touch was all it took to set raw desire burning between them.

"Then it's settled." Silence fell for a moment, then he asked, "Did you miss me?"

She took a deep shuddering breath. There was no point in lying. He could read the truth in her face all too easily. "Yes." Looking up, she saw a gleam of satisfaction in his eyes.

"Good. It's a start."

He was very close to her now. So close she could feel the passion and need burning in him.

"It's dangerous..."

He took her hand and placed it on his chest. Under her flattened palm, beneath the soft flannel shirt, his heart hammered, fast and strong.

"Don't talk to me about danger, Sabrina." His voice was soft and husky above her. "Can't you feel what you do to me? And that's only part of it. Do you need more evidence?"

The blood was singing in her ears as he moved even nearer, until his hips pressed so close, she could feel the contours of his body through their clothing, feel him hard and aroused against her stomach.

"Hey, Sabrina, wanna go fishing?" Colin's voice sounded behind him.

"Damn!" Michael sucked in his breath in a frustrated groan, then stepped around her and walked toward the end of the dock.

Breathless and shuddering, Sabrina moved automatically to intercept Colin, who was coming toward them carrying a couple of fishing rods and a small cardboard carton.

"Sure, sounds like fun," she answered automatically, her heart pounding a crazy tattoo against her ribs, her awareness still focused acutely on Michael.

"Would you like me to bait your hook for you?" Colin had thrust a rod into her hand and sat down on the edge of the dock. She had to force her attention back to his smiling face.

"No, thanks, I can manage." Her voice wavered, but she produced a sick grin, trying to rein in the wave upon wave of trembling arousal that weakened her knees and made her breasts feel swollen and tight. Trying to repress the deep unsatisfied ache that only the man a few tormenting feet away could soothe.

She had no illusions. If Colin hadn't been here, at this moment they would have been locked together, flesh on flesh, Michael buried deep within her, where she wanted him to be. She would be telling him how much she loved him in the most honest, elemental way, without words.

On shaky legs she sank down onto the dock beside Colin and reached into the carton between them for a fat, writhing worm.

"Are you sure? I know girls aren't very good at this sort of thing."

"Listen here, my young friend." Trying to regain her equilibrium, she adopted a teasing, admonitory tone and waved the worm in front of his face. "If you don't want me to use *you* for bait, you'd better not come out with any more comments like that again."

Michael gave a dry chuckle behind her that sent a little shudder up her spine. "I'd listen to her, son. I think she means it."

"You don't have to tell me what she means. I've known her longer than you have," Colin muttered sullenly under his breath.

"Yes, you have."

Something about the warm abstraction in Michael's voice made her turn to look at him. He had seated himself on the weather-beaten boards, one knee drawn up, and the warm light in his eyes took her breath away.

Pain shot through her finger. "Ouch!" she muttered under her breath. She'd gone and stabbed herself with the hook because she wasn't paying attention. She turned her gaze to her task. Looking at him was dangerous.

"Hey, that's pretty good. Where did you learn to do that?" Colin's voice held surprised admiration as he examined her baited hook.

She laughed at his amazement. "My parents run a fishing resort. I've been baiting hooks since I was old enough to climb into a canoe. I'm not just another pretty face, you know."

"I know that, Sabrina." Colin's meaningful tone wasn't lost on her, and she couldn't prevent herself from glancing at Michael.

His gaze held hers for one intense moment, then turned to his son. "It looks like you could use a little help yourself with that worm." The lazy drawl gave no hint of the tension in his eyes a moment before.

"What do you know about fishing?"

"Quite a lot actually," Michael said evenly, ignoring the customary antagonism.

Out of the corner of her eye she saw him stand up and walk behind her to crouch beside his son. "May I?" He took Colin's hook in hand and expertly began to weave the worm on to it. "I spent a lot of summers here when I was a boy. There was nothing else to do but fish."

"That's funny. Grandma never brought me here. She couldn't stand the place."

"She never brought me here, either. She sent me with my nanny. There you go." He handed the line back to Colin who accepted it awkwardly.

"Thanks," he mumbled, resentful and confused.

"You're welcome." Michael's voice held a note of wistfulness that clutched at her heart. There was dark pain in his face as he looked at his son. Colin turned stubbornly away.

"Is anyone else hungry?"

Sabrina looked up to see Anya coming down the steps to the dock.

"I'm starved." Michael sounded brisk and unruffled. "Why don't I go inside and see what I can throw together?"

"I'll help." Anya smiled at him.

Sabrina jumped to her feet. "Better still, why don't I help Anya with lunch and you stay and fish with my rod?" She glanced at Michael and trembled inwardly at the warmth, the admiration and desire she saw in his face. "I've had too much sun."

He turned to Colin. "Would you mind if I fished with you?"

His son shrugged, his attention on the line where it disappeared into the water. "It's a free country—you can do whatever you want."

Michael took a seat beside him, with a quick glance back to Sabrina. She smiled her encouragement, then turned away.

"I know a great spot to fish but we can only get there by canoe. Would you like me to show it to you?"

Behind her, Michael's voice was so casual, it almost fooled her, but she knew the tension with which he'd be awaiting Colin's answer.

"If you want to" came the offhand reply.

"Let's go, then. We're going to need more bait . . ."

Their voices faded as she and Anya gained the house.

"That was a cute little trick, but I wouldn't hold my breath waiting for a miracle." Anya cocked one ginger eyebrow as she held the screen door open for her to pass through.

"Don't I know it." Sabrina heaved a huge sigh.

"Don't lose heart," Anya replied. "These things take time. At least it's a start."

Through the kitchen window Sabrina watched a red canoe nosing out of the boathouse and then gliding away, Michael paddling with impressive expertise.

PERHAPS MIRACLES DID happen after all. That evening at dinner, Colin was more relaxed and exuberant in his father's company than she had ever seen him before. They seemed to be reaching out to each other, even if their progress was halting and tentative.

And it continued the next day. She watched them fishing together off the dock, watched Colin's absorbed fascination as Michael expertly cleaned and filleted the fish, then built a fire on the beach to cook it. Her heart soared with hope. Maybe this really could be a new beginning for them.

If only she hadn't been so conscious of the expression in Michael's eyes whenever he looked at her. That intense and bittersweet despair. As if his happiness at Colin's coming around was tainted by disappointment over her. Ever since that moment of near insanity on the dock, she'd taken pains never to be alone with him and she could tell he had been hurt by her avoidance.

It was almost midnight when she got out of bed and leaned her elbows on the sill of her bedroom window. Sleep was eluding her completely. She gazed up at the moon, sailing high in a sky of ragged silver clouds, and with a shiver of yearning, she felt the soft night air whisper over her bare arms.

Far below, a movement caught her eye, a pale gleam against the dark trees. Then she saw him clearly—a tall, lean figure walking down over the rocks toward the little beach. Her heart skipped a beat, then began to race. *Michael.*

In one swift movement she turned back into the room, pulled off her nightdress and reached for her jeans and sweatshirt. She was crazy. She'd probably live to regret this. But so what?

As she stepped quietly out the front door, the haunting call of the loon came echoing across the darkened water. Every tiny hair on her arms stood on end. Such a lonely sound. As lonely as she felt. She couldn't bear to spend one more second away from him.

The clouds had thickened, making it hard to see her way. A soft breeze whispered through the pines and rustled the dry birch leaves as she moved carefully down the smooth rocks toward the shore. Suddenly the moon came out again from behind the clouds and she could see him down on the beach. He sat on a piece of driftwood, leaning his elbows on his knees as he looked out at the calm water.

All she could hear was the soft slap of the waves and the hiss of the sand tugging at her feet, slowing her steps as she hurried toward him. Still, and waiting in the moonlight, he turned his head to watch her approach.

At last she stood in front of him, gasping slightly and out of breath, but he remained like a statue, his head turned up to her, waiting.

"All along I've felt that we would only end up unhappy, and hurting each other and maybe that's true, but I'm miserable without you. So if I'm going to be unhappy, I'd rather be unhappy with you. I need you, Michael." The last words came out in a broken sob; then he was on his feet and reaching for her. His arms came around her so tightly, she could hardly breathe.

She could hear the laughter in his voice. "My darling, we're going to be two of the happiest people alive." And when he kissed her she felt his exuberance, his triumph, and responded with an urgent thrill of abandon. Finally he drew back a fraction, his breathing heavy. "Let's go back to the house," he said unsteadily.

"No. There are too many people there." She smiled, deliberately slow and seductive. "I want you to make love to me under the stars, Michael."

An answering smile formed on his lips. In the bright moonlight she could see the gleam of desire in his eyes as he swung her up into his arms. "You asked for it. And you're going to get it."

"Promises, promises." She laughed softly and her breasts tingled in delicious anticipation of his threat as he carried her back from the beach, in among the trees, to a small clearing that shimmered in the silvery light. Hidden away from the world, the scene had an unearthly beauty, but then his warm lips met hers again and the world was forgotten.

She clung tightly, arching her body toward his, her arms around his neck, never breaking contact as he slowly lowered her to the ground, until she could feel the soft cushiony moss beneath her shoulders.

He knelt beside her and looked at her lying there, stretched out in the dappled shade, abandoned and primitive, her eyes filled with languid sensuality.

"Through all these endless waiting weeks you've been with me constantly. Did you know that?" he murmured.

A great surge of hunger went through him and he slowly pushed up her sweatshirt, then caught his breath on a gasp as the silver light shaded the curves of her small bare breasts. He leaned closer. The very scent of her flesh was so pure and sweet, so heady, it made him weak with desire.

"In my thoughts, in my dreams." With a trembling finger he traced the line of her rib cage, her skin so smooth and soft. Could anything feel softer? "Tormenting me."

Then he slowly circled the fingertip around one nipple, fascinated as it tightened under his touch.

"Oh, Michael," she breathed, her luscious lips parting slightly with little panting sighs as his hands drifted over her ribs, his thumbs brushing the taut peaks of her breasts.

"You're beautiful. I need to make love with you again, Sabrina."

"Well, then, what are you waiting for, you big dope?" But her voice was a lazily sensual invitation and she arched toward him with a small smile.

Red-hot hunger tore through him. He wanted to possess her, to slowly and thoroughly discover her, enjoying every heavenly minute. That kind of bliss could make up for a lifetime of frustrated waiting.

"I never knew that making love could be like this. I'm overwhelmed—my heart is pounding so hard, I'm afraid it'll stop beating. I've never felt this way with anyone before...."

"I can't believe it."

He could see the doubt in her pale face. "Believe it," he said fervently. "No one's *ever* made me feel this way. No one's ever loved me the way you do. I want you to feel the same."

With agonizing restraint he slowly lowered his head to take one tightly budded nipple into his mouth. But as soon as his lips touched her soft fragrant skin, she let out a little sigh of pleasure and contentment. "Oh, don't stop."

It almost sent him over the edge. "I've only just begun," he groaned against her burning flesh.

Sabrina closed her eyes, giving herself over to the ecstasy he could create with just the simple touch of his mouth. The silky friction of his tongue, twirling and suckling on the nipple, greedy and a little rough, sent pleasure pulsing through her, intensifying the sweet, aching pressure between her thighs.

"Michael?" She cupped his face, raised it to look up at her. In one motion she deliberately grazed her breast against his rough cheek, and caught her breath at the sensation.

"Yes?" Resting on one elbow, he slid a hand through her silky hair and drew one leg over her body, pressing himself against her until it almost hurt. "What is it?"

She arched toward him with a small provocative smile. "Nothing. I just wanted to say your name."

He sighed, and his warm breath shivered along her flesh. "You make me feel very special."

His trembling hands slowly made their way down over her stomach to release the button of her jeans and slowly slide the zipper down.

"Now I want to make you feel very good." He moved lower to place soft, moist kisses on the quivering flesh around her navel.

She looked down at his dark head, lustrous in the moonlight and felt a shuddering erotic thrill at his enjoyment of her body.

"It's my turn." At her murmur he raised his head with a questioning look. "It's my turn to play."

She pushed herself up into a sitting position and Michael sank back on his haunches. Rising to her knees, she reached out to unbutton his shirt. He just knelt there watching her with burning intensity and a small smile on his lips.

With the last button undone, she pulled the shirt out of his pants and pushed it open to splay her hands over his chest. His skin felt so supple and silken, so hot against her palms. Slowly she caressed the smooth muscled contours, brushing his nipples. His muscles flexed involuntarily beneath her touch. He was too irresistible.

She leaned forward to take one of his nipples into her mouth, where it instantly tightened into a hard, tiny little bud. A hunger she didn't know she possessed made her ravish it with her tongue, her lips, her teeth.

With a quick, sharp, almost painful gasp, he sucked in his breath. She glanced up to see his head thrown back, the strong column of his throat exposed to the silver light. With a groan she surged up, unable to resist pressing her lips against the warm flesh of his neck.

Reaching down, she spread her hand over the hard bulge in the front of his pants and felt an instant surge of heat tighten low in her belly as he thrust himself against her.

It was like a pagan ritual in the moonlight. The rhythmic rush of the water, the breeze sighing through the leaves and the small murmured groans of desire.

His hands feverishly caressed her breasts, her skin. She slipped her hand beneath his waistband and her fingers closed around his hard, smooth length. His sharp hiss became a groan of pure pain that brought a smile to her lips as she caressed him with slow, excruciating strokes.

He suddenly grasped her hand. "If you keep that up I'll ruin a perfectly good pair of jeans."

She heard the choked laughter in his voice and murmured, "So what? You can afford another."

With that she shoved him back so that he toppled over, until he was resting on his elbows, legs stretched out in front of him. With impatient, rough hands she yanked his jeans down far enough to expose his erection.

Never, ever had she been so utterly abandoned, but she wanted to give him ecstasy, to see his face and know that he felt the way she did when he did this to her.

Unbounded love for him flowed through every vein as her hand curved around him, sliding back and forth on his velvety smoothness.

A soft anguished groan came from his throat. "Enough." On a sharp breath he pulled her up and took her mouth in a famished, feverish kiss, rolling her underneath him at the same time.

"But I wanted more," she breathed against his lips.

"And you're going to get more." He gave her a smile as his hands slid down her back, until he hooked his thumbs into the waistband of her jeans and pulled them off, so that they were pressed, flesh to flesh. "Much more," he said as he rolled over again and his strong hands lifted her into position above him.

Her groan mingled with a sigh as she slid down over him, her body opening and enfolding him as if she had waited all her life for this moment.

Moving together, their lips joined, she felt his hands everywhere, caressing, cupping her breasts, his fingers teasing the nipples until she was writhing in ecstasy.

"I've never felt this way with any woman before," he gasped against her lips. "I want this night to go on forever."

When his release came, she clung to him, shuddering, but he kept on moving in her until she finally cried out as waves of convulsive pleasure swamped her. Finally she collapsed on him, resting her forehead against his, feeling her heartbeat slow with his.

Her tongue darted out to lick his lips. The erotic gesture made him shudder. With a soft laugh he murmured, "You're bad...."

She allowed her fingers to trail delicately over his chest, loving the feel of his satiny skin, the hardness of his nipples, the way his body reacted to her touch. "And you're delicious," she responded, slightly shocked once again by her boldness. Perhaps it was the moonlight. But whatever it was, she never wanted the magic to end.

For a long time only the soft lapping of the water broke the silence. But all too soon the breeze freshened, creeping through the pines to chill her heated flesh.

His fingers traced over the goose bumps on her thigh. "I think it's time we got dressed."

She sat up and he reached for her sweatshirt. She felt too utterly spent with pleasure to do anything but watch him as he helped her into her clothing, a smile plastered across her face.

Finally, hand in hand, they wandered back out onto the beach, and made their way slowly up toward the house. Michael pulled her against him as they walked. She leaned her head on his shoulder and put her arm around his waist. It felt so right, so natural to be there.

"Well, Sabrina, where do we go from here?"

She raised her head to look up at him, but she didn't know what to say. His face was so serious and intent on her.

"I'm not going to let you tell me that there's no future in this for us...."

"Michael..."

He stopped in front of the cottage and turned toward her, holding her hands. "Sabrina, you can't deny what's happening between us. My God, what happened back there wasn't just sex, a roll in the hay."

She giggled. "Well, it was sort of a roll in the grass."

He broke into an unwilling smile. "Will you be serious?"

Then he curved a hand around her chin and stared down into her eyes. The smile left his face, replaced by something more intense as he lowered his head to hers. "Never mind," he murmured against her lips. "We'll be serious later."

For a long time only the soft whisper of the wind broke the silence as she wrapped her arms around his neck and clung to him in a warm, possessive kiss.

"What are you doing? What's going on here?"

Sabrina froze at the sound of Colin's strangled voice.

10

MICHAEL JERKED AWAY from her while Sabrina could only stare at Colin's stricken face, icy pale in the moonlight.

"How could you?" The words tore out of him. "You did this on purpose to hurt me."

"Colin . . . son."

"Don't you call me son." His fine-drawn features contorted in revulsion.

"Let's just calm down and discuss this." Michael reached for him, but Colin flinched away from his father's outstretched hands.

"No . . ." He shook his head. "No. All my life you never really wanted me. It was all an act to ease your guilty conscience."

"That's not true."

"Yes, it is. My grandmother told me so."

Michael squeezed his eyelids closed and turned away for a moment with such an agonized expression that Sabrina felt as if she'd been stabbed in the heart. When he opened his eyes again she caught the gleam of tears.

"Your grandmother was mistaken." His voice was very quiet but she heard the devastation, saw it in his face.

Her throat tightened and she swallowed hard. How could Sybil have done something so hateful to her own son?

"Then you came back, expecting to change my life around because that's the way you want it. And now this.

You don't care about Sabrina. You just want her because I'm in love with her."

She gasped and quickly looked at Michael, to see him staring at his son, stricken. Moving between them, she reached out and put a hand on Colin's forearm. Beneath her fingers she could feel him taut and trembling.

"Colin, you know that's not true. You're not in love with me."

He dragged his gaze away from his father's face and looked down at her. Something in his chilled expression tore her apart. "No, Sabrina. You're the one who doesn't want to accept it. Why? Because I'm just a kid and I can't fall in love or have any feelings?"

She became aware that tears were rolling down her cheeks. "I don't think that at all. Of course you have feelings. But maybe what you think is love is—"

"No, I don't want to listen to any more. How could you do this to me, Sabrina? I'll never forgive you. Never. I'll hate you both till the day I die." He choked out the last word on a sob, then turned and began running, stumbling down the rocks toward the beach.

Sabrina went to follow. "I should talk to him." Then she felt Michael's trembling hand on her arm.

"Let him go. He needs time to think. And then I should be the one to talk to him."

"Of course. You're right." She took a deep breath as she turned to him, wiping the tears from her cheeks with the back of her hand. "What a mess. How are we going to convince Colin that he doesn't really love me?"

He slowly shook his head, never taking his anguished gaze from hers. "How are we going to convince Colin that *I* love you, and I want to marry you?"

For a moment she could only stare up at his features, lean and shadowed in the moonlight, before whispering, "Marry?"

He framed her face with his long fingers, tenderly stroking her damp cheekbones with his thumbs as he smiled down at her with gentle mockery. "Of course, marry. What do you think this has been about all this time?"

Her vision blurred as her eyes filled with tears again. She covered his hands with hers and shook her head slightly. "But why me, Michael?"

"Why you? Because I've never met anyone like you before. Your bravery, your reckless sense of loyalty, your generous heart . . . your sweetness."

"So far, you make me sound like a Boy Scout." She gave a shaky laugh.

"And then when I'm near you . . ." He let out a deep breath as if he didn't know where to begin. "It's like I go up in flames. And when I kiss you, it's like I've never been kissed before. Do you know what it's like to be in a business meeting, being asked a question I can't answer because I'm thinking about you? Or even worse, sitting there with a hard-on. Do you know what that's like?"

She had to laugh through the tears. "Not really."

"Oh, you think it's funny, do you?" He smiled, but then he sobered. "If you don't marry me soon, I'll go out of my mind." He began covering her face with small kisses, murmuring, "And you're too sweet and generous to allow that to happen."

Was this really happening, or would she wake any second to find it had only been a cruel, heartbreaking dream?

Suddenly the brutal roar of a powerful motor tore through the silence.

Michael jerked upright. "Colin!" he exclaimed, his voice as sharp and rigid as his body. And then he was moving away from her so quickly that she reeled from the loss of support of his arms.

By the time she regained her balance and was running after him, Michael had reached the end of the dock, shouting his son's name as the sleek racing vessel shot off over the moonlit water.

She reached him a second later, panting for breath. "Oh, Michael, you don't think he's going to do anything foolish, do you?"

The running lights of the boat became red-and-white sparks in the distance, swiftly disappearing in the direction of the mainland.

"God, I hope not." He turned and strode quickly toward the steps that led up to the house. Sabrina ran after him.

Halfway up they met Anya, still rumpled from sleep and tying the sash of her robe as she hurried down to meet them. "What's happening?"

"No time to explain." Michael broke into a run as he went past her, throwing back the clipped order, "Get packed. We're leaving."

As they followed him up to the cottage, Sabrina told Anya that Colin had gone and she gave a sketchy explanation. They found Michael pacing the living room with his cellular phone clutched tightly against his ear.

"Come on, damn it. Answer."

Sabrina dashed upstairs as she heard him burst into rapid speech. Twenty minutes later, with the sleepy caretaker at the wheel, they were speeding across the lake.

SABRINA HUNG ON to the pole and waited for the rattling streetcar to come to a halt. The back doors creaked open, she stepped out onto the pavement and the cold air hit her face.

Indian summer was over, along with all her hopes and happiness. Hunching her shoulders against the nip in the air, she pushed her hands into her jacket pocket and rushed down University Avenue toward Toronto General Hospital.

Please, God, let Charlie be all right. His daughter Marie had said it was only a mild stroke, and for a man in his late seventies he was in excellent health, but she just couldn't take it if something happened to Charlie, on top of everything else.

Colin hadn't returned home. Michael had called to tell her he would be away for a few days trying to track his son down. Worried sick about them, she'd gone to call Charlie, only to hear from Marie that he'd been taken to hospital. She dashed in the main doors, inquired at the front desk and was directed to a room on the seventh floor.

Her suede boots squeaked on the polished yellow linoleum as she rushed down the corridor. Passing an open doorway, she heard the click of table-tennis balls and a gentle, familiar voice.

"My point, I believe."

She stopped in her tracks and peered in the doorway. The large sunny room had tall windows giving a view of the skyline. In one corner sat a television, facing two couches and several easy chairs, and at the other end of the room stood a Ping-Pong table.

Charlie was dressed in pyjamas and a plaid bathrobe, but he hadn't lost one iota of his distinguished bearing. His snowy hair was carefully brushed, his mustache neatly trimmed.

The short middle-aged man across the table grinned at him. "I'm gonna quit. You've been practising too much."

Charlie caught sight of her standing in the doorway. "Why, Sabrina! I wasn't expecting you back till tonight."

A wave of heartfelt relief swept over her. She'd been terrified of finding Charlie at death's door. And now, to her undying embarrassment, she found herself bursting into tears.

He came over, took her arm and gently led her to his room, past the stares of nurses and other patients. Somehow, after all the emotional turmoil she'd been through, it was all too much.

Charlie settled her in a chair beside the bed, handed her a handkerchief from his pocket and she buried her face in the fresh white cotton. He sank quietly into the other chair and waited calmly for the storm to pass.

After a while she began to regain control, took a deep shaky breath and blew her nose into the handkerchief. "I thought you were dying. I rush over here and what do I find? You're playing table tennis of all things!"

"Sorry to disappoint you."

She batted the handkerchief at him and laughed weakly as fresh tears coursed down her cheek. "You know what I mean."

He poured a glass of water from the jug by the bed and handed it to her. "Are you feeling any better now?"

She took a sip, hiccuped and nodded. "Charlie, don't you ever do that to me again."

Taking the glass from her, he patted her hand. "There, there, girlie. Everything's fine."

"This has been the worst weekend of my life."

"The holiday didn't work out too well?"

"That's an understatement. And then you go and pull a stunt like this!"

"Now, now. Don't go getting yourself all worked up. I'm fine. Tell me about your weekend."

"It's a long story and I won't burden you with all the grisly details right now."

But that was the wrong thing to say to Charlie. After a few gentle questions and perceptive guesses, he had her telling him almost everything.

He didn't offer solutions or pass judgments, just listened. And she realized how much she had needed to pour it all out to someone who cared. Then she resolutely put it aside and concentrated on him.

He was annoyed at his doctor's insistence on more tests; it meant remaining in hospital for a few days when he felt perfectly fine. But Sabrina was glad to know he was getting good care. She left the hospital, promising to return tomorrow and spend as many hours with him as visiting time allowed.

The rest of the day passed without a word from Michael and on Monday morning she hurried to work, hoping against hope that he might be there, but once again she was disappointed. What could be happening? Had he found Colin?

It was hard to keep her mind on work as she stood on top of a ladder, hanging the final snowflakes around Santa's Castle. The area was closed off until the day of the parade, and there was no one there except herself and two workmen laying the red carpet that led up to Santa's throne. It was too quiet, with no distractions from her worried thoughts.

Suddenly the ladder jolted beneath her and began to tip. At the same moment she heard a surprised grunt from below.

"You fool, why don't you watch where you're going!" she yelled, grabbing for the foam snowflake, but it came away in her hand.

Wildly she threw her weight in the opposite direction, and the ladder tipped back upright. But her foot slipped on the tread, she lost her balance and went sliding down the side of the rungs, the friction burning her knees through her pants. She landed hard on something wide and padded.

Angry and shaken, she looked down between her thighs to see a round red face, jowls quivering in outrage like a Tom turkey.

"Oh my God, Mr. Stevenson!"

"Miss Cates." He could hardly spit out her name. "Get off me instantly!" But she was already scrambling to get down off his shoulders, which wasn't easy because he didn't help one bit. She slid sideways, trying to get one leg on the floor, but somehow ended up dangling upside down.

"Miss Cates, have you gone crazy!" he spluttered, trying to pry her legs off his shoulders.

Sabrina clutched at his thighs. "Stop it, you're going to drop me on my head, you fool!" she screamed, then clamped her lips shut as she realized what she'd just called him.

But at that same moment she noticed a foreign object clutched in her hand, something small, gray and furry. She squealed and flung it away, losing her grip and sliding off the rest of the way to land in a heap on the floor.

"What is the meaning of this outrageous behavior?" Walter's voice tightened to a venomous hiss. "Miss Cates, you are the most incompetent, insubordinate, clumsy, stupid, irritating, pestilential employee it has ever been my misfortune to run across!"

Dimly aware of the two carpet layers staring at them in shock, Sabrina sat up, a little dazed. Shaking her head to clear it, she looked up and her eyes widened in horror.

Then she put a hand to her mouth as laughter burst out of her.

He was bald, completely bald, his bumpy head shining under the lights like a waxed turnip. That furry thing he was stepping on must be his wig.

"Stand up and explain yourself, Miss Cates," he barked.

With pleasure. She yanked the toupee out from under his foot, making him stumble a little, and got to her feet.

Choking back the laughter, she schooled her face into the blandest expression she could manage and handed him the object, held fastidiously between thumb and forefinger. "I believe this is yours, sir."

He looked at the wig, then up at her, the veins in his forehead bulging. Snatching it from her hand without a word, he turned and stalked out of the department. The workmen burst into a chorus of snickering as he passed by and she couldn't help but laugh, too.

Oh, Lord, she'd probably lose her job over this one. Then the laughter died in her throat as reality came crashing back in on a sudden wave of anxiety. Right now, her job was the least of her worries.

MICHAEL CALLED that evening to tell her that Colin was back home after staying with a friend. He was going to try and talk to his son, now that Colin had had some breathing space.

All day Tuesday there was no sign of Michael at work. By evening she couldn't stand it any longer and went up to the executive suite. The reception area was empty, but his door stood open. She walked in to see Colin dropping some papers on his father's desk. He would have brushed right past, but she stopped him with a hand on his arm.

"Please, don't leave. We need to talk."

He refused to turn and look at her. "I really have to get going. I've got stacks of homework to do."

"You can't keep avoiding me forever."

"I don't think there's anything to talk about."

This frigid rejection was unbearable. "Don't cut me out. We've been such good friends. I know I hurt you but—"

"I made a fool of myself." He stood rigid, his voice stiff and formal. "There's no need to remind me of it. I really don't want to discuss it."

It broke her heart to see him like this, a hurt boy trying desperately hard for adult dignity.

"But *I* do. I need to get a few things off my chest."

"Why? To ease your conscience?" He finally shifted his gaze to meet hers. The disillusion filling his eyes cut her like a knife. "Okay, go ahead."

"I never meant to hurt you, because I love you. I've always loved you as a very special friend. I thought you would outgrow your feelings for me."

A spasm of pain passed over his face. "I tried to tell you how I felt, but you just laughed me off. I was just a dumb kid. Well, I'm not a dumb kid, Sabrina. Everybody grows up sooner or later. I've grown up, too. You just didn't want to see it. You said you were my friend. You *said* you cared, but you never... I was just a nuisance to you, wasn't I?"

"That's not true."

He shook his head bitterly. "You don't have to pretend anymore. Did you think I wouldn't be able to figure it out about you and Michael? Were you going to keep it a secret, or didn't I count in your future plans at all? You know, Sabrina, you taught me a valuable lesson about relationships, about life."

"You're seventeen years old for heaven's sake! Ten years from now you'll be thinking back on all this and wondering how you could ever—"

"No, I won't!" The words exploded out of him, then he lowered his voice. "I'm not like you, Sabrina. And I'm not like Michael. I'm me."

She fell silent for a moment. He was right. Neither she nor his father had the power to tell him how to feel. Things had changed between them, never to be the same again.

"I feel totally responsible for everything that's happened." She swallowed hard over the lump in her throat. "I'm so sorry. I never meant to hurt you."

"No!"

Michael stepped in through the doorway and saw Sabrina and Colin turn sharply at the sound of his voice. Sabrina looked distraught, her eyes filled with tears. He wanted to go to her, put his arms around her, comfort her, but now was not the time. Colin needed him more, in spite of the cold anger in his son's face that pierced his heart like a knife.

"No," he repeated. "If anybody should take the blame, it should be me."

He stepped toward his son, but the boy moved back from him, distrusting, and gave a mirthless laugh.

"It's funny, the two of you both so anxious to assume responsibility. As far as I'm concerned, you can both go to hell. I'm sick of you trying to make me believe that you care about me."

Hopelessness and desperation made a tight hard lump in Michael's chest. How could he get this boy to understand?

He swallowed hard. "What can I do to convince you that I love you and I always have, and everything I ever did was motivated by your needs?"

Colin gave a snort of disbelief.

"I know it makes no sense to you," Michael continued, "but it's the truth."

"The truth is that you did the easiest thing for yourself."

He wasn't getting through. Michael squeezed his hand into a fist and felt the fast painful thudding of his heart against his ribs. Somewhere inside, cold black fear overwhelmed him. This could be the last chance he'd ever get to reach his son.

He took a deep, unsteady breath. "You have to understand, I was not much older than you are now. I barely had the means to support you...." Colin groaned and half turned away. "...And you needed me."

"And you resented me." Colin rounded on him again, angry and accusatory.

"Resented you? No. Scared to death? Yes. What did I know about babies? For that matter, what did I know about life?"

He paused, praying that his son would meet his eyes, wanting to make him see how it had been. He didn't expect forgiveness or exoneration. He'd been wrong. But he desperately needed his son to understand why he did what he did.

"So am I supposed to feel sorry for you now?"

Michael felt the dull chill of defeat settle over him and gave a slow painful shake of his head. "I'm not saying for a moment that I didn't do wrong. I made some terrible mistakes where you were concerned, but you have to understand that I made them out of love for you, not because I didn't care."

"Okay, fine. I can understand that when I was a baby. But later..."

"When you were four I wanted you to come and live with me, but I let your grandmother convince me that it would be cruel to take you away from the only home you'd ever known. Better to wait till you were a little older, she said."

"Are you trying to tell me she deliberately kept us apart?" Colin glared at him in disgust, as if Michael were trying any low tactic to win his point. "She knew how much I wanted you. I used to cry for you." His voice hardened in accusation. "But Grandma told me you were too busy, you wouldn't want to be saddled with a kid...."

Sabrina sucked in her breath in shocked disbelief.

Michael's eyes burned with pain and anger. "That's not true!" His voice broke as he repeated, "That's not true."

She knew the man that she loved. He was too honorable to get himself off the hook by exposing his mother as a cruel liar, and he loved his son too much to inflict even more hurt. Aching with pride and love for Michael, she felt impotent, desperate to ease his pain, but knowing there was nothing she could do.

"I never knew you cried for me. I never guessed," Michael said huskily. "You resented me so much."

"And I suppose you blamed me?"

Michael shook his head slowly. "No, I never blamed you. I blamed myself."

Suddenly the adult hardness vanished from Colin's face. He looked like a lost little boy as his lips compressed and tears filled his eyes. Michael began to move toward him, but Colin swiftly shook his head and held up a hand to ward him off. Michael stopped in his tracks.

Across the space of three feet, father and son stared at each other. Sabrina felt a lump in her throat. It might as well be the deepest chasm or the width of an ocean. Here in this room stood the two people she loved most in this world, her every hope for happiness, and now she was watching it all crumble into dust.

"Is there nothing I can do or say that would make this up to you?"

"No, nothing." With a strangled sob, Colin brushed past him and left the room.

Michael stood for a long, still moment, then slowly walked toward his desk, pain and anger and futility etching every line of his handsome face. Suddenly he picked up the file lying on the desktop, turned with savage fury and hurled it against the wall.

As the scattered papers fluttered to the floor, he leaned on the desk and sank his forehead onto his hand, looking so utterly defeated that Sabrina couldn't bear it.

"I never asked her for her love," his hollow voice expressionless, every vestige of emotion drained out of him, "because I knew from my earliest childhood that she had none to give me. But I didn't deserve her hate."

It was the ugliest thing she had ever heard. "She was your mother! How could she not love her child?"

"She couldn't love anyone. Maybe it had something to do with my grandfather's suicide—I never fully understood—but Sybil thought emotional ties made you weak and vulnerable. And for a Worth, nothing could be worse. She made sure I never formed any as a child. As soon as I became attached to a nanny, she would be replaced."

"But what about your father? What did he have to say about all of this?"

"I didn't know my father. He died when I was two. And when I asked about him, Sybil told me he was an old man when she married him. She needed money and Worth's needed an heir. She didn't leave me with too many illusions. She didn't even give me his name. I was a Worth, and nothing else mattered. She used him like she used everyone else, and she wanted to turn me into someone just like her."

"But you're not." She came up behind him and wrapped her arms around his waist, laying her cheek against the fine navy wool covering his back.

Michael expelled a heavy breath and turned to wrap his arms around her. She could feel him trembling as he buried his face in her hair, holding her so tightly, she could barely breathe. But she didn't mind. How desperately she wished she could absorb his pain. Why couldn't they just forget who they were? Find themselves far away, without a past, and just go on together.

He spoke against her hair. "I've decided I'm going to take Colin away for a holiday. Just him and I. I made the arrangements this morning."

"That's a wonderful idea, Michael." But she knew what she had to do, and gently pushed herself away from him. "You have to keep on trying with Colin. You can't give up." He nodded in agreement. She swallowed hard and continued. "But I think that to make things easier, I have to leave."

For a moment he was completely still, hardly breathing, as he looked at her with a blank expression in his eyes; then she saw the horror dawn on his face. "No!" The word tore out of him and his lean fingers dug into the flesh of her upper arms so tightly, she knew they'd be bruised. "No. What are you saying?"

"What about Colin?"

His soothing hands stroked over her back. "We'll talk to him. Everything will work out."

"There's no guarantee of a happy-ever-after ending. This isn't a fairy tale. It doesn't have to work out."

For a moment he said nothing; then she felt him stiffen and clutch her to him even more tightly.

"Sabrina, what are we saying? How can we contemplate sacrificing our happiness like this? Let's just get married. Things will *have* to work out."

Her voice emerged thick and husky with unshed tears. "We can't start our marriage like that. What if Colin never comes around? How happy can we be, knowing we've estranged your son for life?"

"I can't let you leave." His eyes filled with a wild mixture of fear and pain.

But there was no other way, and he knew it, too. She felt the tears perilously close, but fought them back ferociously. She had to be calm. And she had to be strong.

"I've been thinking it over and we have no other choice. My being here will only complicate things between you and Colin."

"But what will you do? Where will you go?"

She hadn't even given it a thought. If she didn't have Michael, it didn't matter. But she didn't want him worrying about her. "Don't you think I could get myself another job?" she asked, rallying a smile. "As a matter of fact, the competition's been after me for years, trying to get me over to their side." The desperate try for humor failed miserably.

"Whatever I can do to help—"

She quickly cut him off. "Don't worry about me, Michael. I'll be fine."

He was gripping her arms so tightly, they were aching now. He didn't want to let her go, but she could see in his eyes that he knew there was no other way. "Sabrina..."

There was so much longing and desperation in that one word it almost tore her apart. "You know I'm right, Michael. You know it's the only way." Despite her effort to fight them back, the tears spilled over onto her cheeks—

silent, slow and hot. "You two go away and get things sorted out. Then, when you come back . . ."

"When we come back I'm going to come looking for you."

She nodded. *If you still want me. If you still need me.*

His grip relaxed on her arms, but he began caressing her flesh gently with his fingers, as if he couldn't bear to break the contact.

"When will you go?" His voice cracked, raw and husky with emotion.

"After the parade. I'll leave then." She wiped at the warm, salty tears that had found their way to the corners of her mouth.

He took a deep breath and straightened, seeming to rally a little. "I'm not giving up on us, Sabrina. You said yourself that Colin will come around, and when he does, I'm coming after you," he said fiercely. "Will you wait for me?"

She stared up and saw the despair and hope in his eyes, loving him with all her heart and soul. "Forever," she whispered.

But she felt a deep shudder of foreboding. It could very well be forever. But there would never be anyone else for her. She loved Michael. Time and distance could never change that.

He took her into his arms and she clung to him. His eyes traced her features, as if he wanted to commit them to memory. Then, with a small anguished sound he lowered his head to kiss her.

For a few blissful moments she allowed her lips to cling to his, helpless to stop the silent tears from pouring down her face. She could taste them on her lips as she forced herself to pull away from him, from the anguish in his eyes that mirrored the pain in her heart.

She turned blindly away. He still held on to her hand as it slid through his, and she knew they could both hardly bear to break that last contact. Fingertips grazed, holding for a second, and then she turned and left him behind.

LIFE BECAME REDUCED to an endless tunnel of misery. As she counted down the hours until the parade, Sabrina almost thanked God for the twelve-hour days that kept her running, solving one last-minute crisis after another.

But the nights were terrible, long dark sleepless hours of trying not to think about Michael. Trying to forget how he looked those few times she had caught sight of him in the store. He never smiled anymore. All the joy had gone out of his life. She could see it in his drawn face. He looked older, the lines beside his mouth etched a little deeper.

Now, too late, she finally understood the depth and source of the loneliness that haunted him. His mother had been incapable of love, his son resented him and his wife had used him. How could a man live that kind of life and be expected to know about love?

And yet he had an abundance of love inside him to give, and she felt proud that he had chosen to give it to her. But now, circumstances were forcing her to repeat the loveless pattern of his life. She, too, had to push him away. If she didn't love him so much, she'd never be able to do it. But knowing that she was doing it for him didn't stop her heart from breaking.

In the midst of all her misery, she had one thing to be grateful for. After a battery of tests, the doctors had let Charlie go home. But despite his clean bill of health, there was no way he could be Santa this year, and she found an ally in his daughter Marie. Although he'd apparently made a complete recovery, they both feared the excitement would be too taxing for him.

She wouldn't endanger her dearest friend, even if he was the only Santa Claus she could ever imagine. So she'd asked George from the seniors' center to fill in, having forgiven him for the fiasco of the protest.

And now finally the day was here, after all the months of planning and hard work. The first Saturday in November dawned cold and gray, threatening snow from low, fast-moving clouds. By one o'clock in the afternoon, she was standing on the pavement in front of the store, watching the floats come in.

The Owl and the Pussycat, Mother Goose, Sleeping Beauty... fairy tales and nursery rhymes, childhood fantasies, they rolled on, one after another. Here came the clowns in their orange-and-white polka dots, followed by a rolling big top with an animated tiger jumping through a flaming ring. From somewhere up Yonge Street, hidden by the crowd, came the brassy strains of the next marching band.

The cold air nipped her cheeks and she shoved her chilled hands into the pockets of her coat. Winter had suddenly sprung upon them, as it did so often in Ontario. Hard to believe a week ago she had been enjoying the warmth of an Indian summer.

Her first parade. This should be the happiest moment of her life. Over the walkie-talkies she had heard from the marshals that the new floats were wildly popular. People were saying it was the best parade they'd seen in years. It should have been her moment of triumph, but all she felt was pain and sadness. She felt almost detached from it all.

A stir in the crowd made her turn to see the big front doors open, and she felt her constant pain sharpen into needles of despair.

Michael emerged to stand on the steps, along with a group of civic dignitaries, and behind them ranged the gray flannel retinue. He mustn't see her, so she moved away, trying to lose herself in the crowd massed by the street corner.

A few flakes of snow were beginning to drift down as she edged through the families clustered by the roadside. Tiny children lined the curb, bundled up against the cold in snowsuits and scarves so that only their eyes peeked out, alight with anticipation.

From the street vendors' carts came the tang of roasted chestnuts and barbecued hot dogs. People were cheering the floats, singing along with the marching bands, smiling and talking to strangers. The friendliness and spirit of goodwill were almost tangible and brought a lump to her throat.

One of the marshals walking by flashed her the thumbs-up sign. "Looking great! Well done, Sabrina. Good job!"

She smiled at him, but it was only a movement of her lips. Nothing meant anything anymore. Not even this.

Her eyes kept seeking Michael, as if just the sight of him were balm to her wounded soul. But his face was the saddest face she'd ever seen. She melted farther into the crowd, feeling cold, bleak misery. Suddenly a hand grabbed her elbow from behind.

Shock trembled through her at the sight of Colin's face. He gave her a small, uncertain smile. "Hi."

"Hi," she responded automatically, stunned that he had deliberately approached her. But at the same time a tiny little germ of hope lodged itself in her heart. She held her breath.

"Great parade." A little stiff and awkward, he nodded toward the passing cluster of ladybugs and butterflies.

"Yeah, it seems to have worked out." Breathless, she felt her heart speeding up.

His eyes met hers for a moment, then slid away, but not before she saw the anxiety there, the uncertainty, and the hope inside her grew a little more.

"I had a visit from Santa last night."

"Oh?" Against all reason, the hope was growing inside her by leaps and bounds, tightening in her chest and throat until she felt almost strangled.

"Yeah. We had a long talk." He looked down into her eyes again. "Want to know what we talked about?"

"Uh-huh." She nodded, a convulsive little jerk of her head.

"He asked me what I wanted for Christmas."

"And what did you say?" She had to force her voice to stay calm and even, trying to contain her breathless anxiety.

His gaze slid away again. She saw him swallow hard, and when he looked back at her, his eyes were shining, his voice sounded thick and tremulous. "I told him I wanted my dad." A tear trickled down his cheek and suddenly he looked so young, so vulnerable. Just a boy. "That's what I've wanted for such a long, long time."

With an inarticulate cry, she put her arms around him and led him through the crowd, back against the wall of the building, away from the curious looks. Her own tears were flowing freely as she hugged him tight.

"Oh, Colin, he loves you so much. Just give him a chance. All he wants is to *be* your dad." She stepped back and looked up into his face as he wiped a hand across his cheeks.

"I've been a real idiot, haven't I?" She shook her head, but he went on seriously. "Yes I have. I tried to punish you, because I thought you were trying to take my father away just when we were getting closer."

"Nobody could come between you and your father. He loves you so much."

"I know that now. Can you ever forgive me?"

In answer, she hugged him again, not sure whether to laugh or cry, but doing both at the same time. She could feel him shaking as he hugged her back.

"Come on." Colin put her away from him with determination and took her hand in a firm grip.

"Where are we going?" She sniffed and fished a tissue from her pocket, trying to keep up as he pulled her through the crowd.

"This isn't finished yet." Radiating resolution and pent-up excitement, he gave her a look that made her catch her breath. "Aren't we forgetting someone?"

No. She had never forgotten for a second. He began fighting his way through the closely packed crowd, pulling her along behind him. She was too short to see anything up ahead; she could just make out a blur of hats and winter coats, and the legs of children riding on their father's shoulders for a better look.

Suddenly Colin stopped, moved aside and pulled her forward. She found herself at the main entrance again and looked up to see Michael three steps above her. His grave face was focused on the passing parade, but she could tell from his expression that he really wasn't seeing anything at all.

She opened her mouth to say his name, but nothing came out; then suddenly he turned and looked down at her. The blank look vanished as he frowned, his gaze shifting to Colin, slightly behind her. She turned to see Colin smiling up at his father, shy, uncertain, but determined nevertheless. Michael stared back at him as if he didn't dare trust his own eyes.

He took the first two stairs slowly, like a man in a dream, then almost leapt down the last step to sweep his son into an embrace.

With his father's arms around him, Colin bit his lip nervously. "I love you, Dad. I'm sorry I've been such a jerk."

Michael heaved a massive sigh and closed his eyes, gripping his son as if he never wanted to let him go. "I love you more than life itself."

Sublime, inexpressible happiness filled her heart. This moment had been a long time coming. The wounds of the past couldn't be healed overnight, but now they could heal together, father and son at last.

Michael released the boy with one arm and turned toward her, the lines of fear and care smoothed from his face as he reached out to pull her into his embrace, but she held back.

Colin gave them both a challenging grin. "I hope you guys plan on marrying soon. It's time we became a real family."

Michael met his son's smile and laughed, carefree and happy. "Don't you worry about that. Will a special license be soon enough for you?"

"Wait a minute!" Her sober expression made them both stop smiling. "I think you should stick to your original plan."

Michael stared at her in confusion.

"Maybe it isn't a good idea to rush into this. You need time with your son to make up for all those wasted years, time to think about what you really want."

The bewilderment vanished from his face and that hard, implacable mask closed over it again, daunting her, but she knew what she had to do.

"You and Colin should go away...."

"We'll all go away together." His tone was uncompromising.

"Then, when you come back—"

"I'm not letting you go, Sabrina," Michael broke in. "I won't let you talk yourself out of this. I love you, and you love me. I know you do."

"I do. I do love you, but..."

"No buts. I want to marry you, Sabrina. I want your answer now and it had better be yes."

Once again she faced that hard, indomitable man she had first encountered.

"Aw, come on, lady. Put the poor guy out of his misery—say yes."

At the strange voice, she turned with a start to find that the surrounding crowd were all looking at *them*, not the parade. Even Walter Stevenson stood gaping down at them from the top step, his mouth hanging open in astonishment.

Looking to Colin she saw only eager encouragement. Her gaze came back to Michael, who only watched her steadily. There was no pleading in his eyes now. He just waited.

And then someone in the crowd started chanting, "Say yes. Say yes."

Before long, a multitude of other voices had joined in. But the quiet, waiting look in Michael's eyes held her mesmerized.

Then another voice yelled out, "Give the girl a chance. He wouldn't hear her even if she did say yes."

And then there was silence. Vaguely she became aware of another marching band going by, and still Michael watched her with that steady look.

What choice did she have? Who was she to argue with fate when it was offering to make all her dreams come true? A slow smile broke out on her face. "Yes."

A cheer went up from the crowd around them. With a triumphant smile, Michael gathered her in his arms, completely uncaring of their audience.

"Just as well. I wasn't going to take no for an answer."

And then his lips met hers in a kiss that left her breathless and clinging to him.

Suddenly she heard Colin call out, "Hey! Here comes Santa!"

Michael lifted his head. With one hot look that promised much more to come later, he led her up to the top step. Walter Stevenson stood back to make room for her, his quivering jowls slack, his mouth hanging open in stupefaction.

Laughter rose to her lips, but then all thoughts of Walter's ludicrous outrage fled from her mind when Michael came to stand behind her. He wrapped her tightly in his arms, molding her to his hard body, as if he couldn't bear to let her go.

Warm and safe in his embrace, she watched the final float approach, a fantasy of glittering ice and snow with little green elves perched along the edge and a massive red sleigh pulled by mechanical reindeer.

A Fairy Tale Christmas she had called the parade this year, and that was how it would be for her. This Christmas and all the rest to come, with Michael at her side.

The only shadow on her perfect happiness was the thought that it wouldn't be Charlie in the sleigh. Nobody else seemed to care. The crowd below exploded in cheers and the children began jumping up and down and waving madly as the float came nearer. She had to hand it to George, though. He was doing a wonderful job.

"Ho, ho, ho" came booming over the speakers. "Merry Christmas!"

And his voice sounded almost exactly like... As the float made its majestic approach, she peered hard at the man in the familiar scarlet costume, at the twinkling gray eyes above the white whiskers, then slowly she shook her head in disbelief.

"It's Charlie!"

The float rolled to a halt in front of the store and Sabrina began cheering and jumping up and down along with the rest of the crowd. "Michael, look, it's Charlie!"

It was Charlie all right, waving and ho-ho-ho-ing to everyone's delight. He caught sight of her on the steps and blew her a kiss. Now everything really was perfect.

"Thanks, Santa," Colin yelled out beside her.

And suddenly she knew who had paid him a visit the night before. Charlie had been Worth's Santa ever since Colin was seven years old. Who would be better than Charlie at helping a confused boy get past his own hurt and see his father for the man he really was—a loving man who made his mistakes while desperately trying to do the right thing.

She had Charlie to thank for setting Colin on the road to a newfound maturity and understanding. She had Charlie to thank for her happiness.

Choked with tears, she blew him a kiss in return. "Yes. Thank you, Santa."

Turning to Michael, she wrapped her arms tightly around him as he looked down into her eyes.

"I love you," he whispered as the crowd went crazy around them.

"And I love you." Her lips met his in a kiss so sweet and filled with so much promise that Sabrina knew with all her heart that there really must be a Santa Claus after all.

MILLION DOLLAR SWEEPSTAKES (III)

No purchase necessary. To enter, follow the directions published. Method of entry may vary. For eligibility, entries must be received no later than March 31, 1996. No liability is assumed for printing errors, lost, late or misdirected entries. Odds of winning are determined by the number of eligible entries distributed and received. Prizewinners will be determined no later than June 30, 1996.

Sweepstakes open to residents of the U.S. (except Puerto Rico), Canada, Europe and Taiwan who are 18 years of age or older. All applicable laws and regulations apply. Sweepstakes offer void wherever prohibited by law. Values of all prizes are in U.S. currency. This sweepstakes is presented by Torstar Corp., its subsidiaries and affiliates, in conjunction with book, merchandise and/or product offerings. For a copy of the Official Rules send a self-addressed, stamped envelope (WA residents need not affix return postage) to: MILLION DOLLAR SWEEPSTAKES (III) Rules, P.O. Box 4573, Blair, NE 68009, USA.

EXTRA BONUS PRIZE DRAWING

No purchase necessary. The Extra Bonus Prize will be awarded in a random drawing to be conducted no later than 5/30/96 from among all entries received. To qualify, entries must be received by 3/31/96 and comply with published directions. Drawing open to residents of the U.S. (except Puerto Rico), Canada, Europe and Taiwan who are 18 years of age or older. All applicable laws and regulations apply; offer void wherever prohibited by law. Odds of winning are dependent upon number of eligibile entries received. Prize is valued in U.S. currency. The offer is presented by Torstar Corp., its subsidiaries and affiliates in conjunction with book, merchandise and/or product offering. For a copy of the Official Rules governing this sweepstakes, send a self-addressed, stamped envelope (WA residents need not affix return postage) to: Extra Bonus Prize Drawing Rules, P.O. Box 4590, Blair, NE 68009, USA.

SWP-H1295

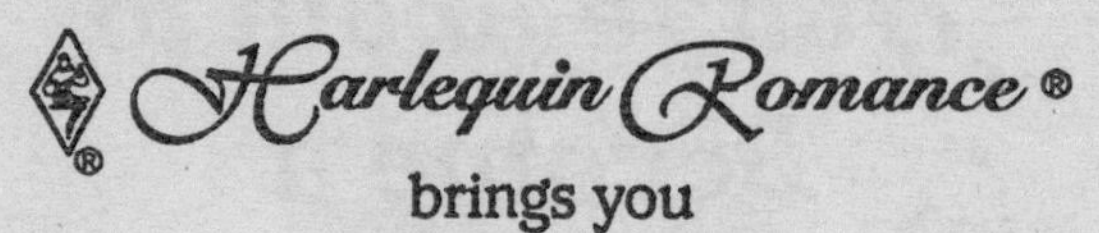

brings you

How the West Was Wooed!

Harlequin Romance would like to welcome you Back to the Ranch again in 1996 with our new miniseries, Hitched! We've rounded up twelve of our most popular authors, and the result is a whole year of romance, Western-style. Every month we'll be bringing you a spirited, independent woman whose heart is about to be lassoed by a rugged, handsome, one-hundred-percent cowboy!

Watch for books branded Hitched! in the coming months. We'll be featuring all your favorite writers including, Patricia Knoll, Ruth Jean Dale, Rebecca Winters and Patricia Wilson, to mention a few!

HITCH-G